Clint Adams had to die . . .

Things had not gone the way Johnny Robak had imagined they would. His legend just was not growing the way he had expected it to.

Damn it, he'd outdrawn the Gunsmith, put the man down fair and square in the street in front of witnesses. What more did they want?

He knew the answer to that one without anyone telling him.

He'd left Clint Adams alive, and people were holding that against him.

He had killed the *legend*, but he had not killed the *man*.

He had to set that right.

Also in the GUNSMITH series

THE GUNSMITH

80

WHEN LEGENDS DIE

J. R. ROBERTS

JOVE BOOKS, NEW YORK

THE GUNSMITH #80: WHEN LEGENDS DIE

A Jove Book / published by arrangement with
the author

PRINTING HISTORY
Jove edition / August 1988

ISBN: 0-515-09685-7

Jove Books are published by The Berkley Publishing Group,
200 Madison Avenue, New York, New York 10016.
The name "JOVE" and the "J" logo
are trademarks belonging to Jove Publications, Inc.

PRINTED IN THE UNITED STATES OF AMERICA

10 9 8 7 6 5 4 3 2 1

PROLOGUE
ZENITH, COLORADO

The girl's breasts bobbed intriguingly before his face as she rode him. Her head was thrown back so he couldn't see her face, but he knew she'd be biting her lip. He was waiting for the time she'd bite that luscious lower lip clean off.

She was young, and her breasts would probably get larger and firmer, but right now he was fascinated by the way they jiggled and bobbed. Her nipples were a light brown, with large aureola, and he knew how sensitive they were. He reached for her and pulled her down so he could reach them with his mouth. He sucked them each in turn, and when he felt her belly beginning to tremble he knew she was on the verge of coming.

Abruptly he flipped her over so that she was on the

bottom and he was on top. He slid his hands beneath her and cupped her well-shaped, firm ass. Her breasts would mature, but for some reason she already had a perfect, fully developed derrière.

He began to pound his huge erection into her and her breath came in great gusts every time he drove it home. Then she was writhing and wriggling beneath him, as if she were trying to get out from under him—but he knew that wasn't the case.

He continued to slam into her, squeezing her buttocks hard in his hands. Finally he swelled and came, filling her with his semen, and she ran her nails down his back without breaking the skin. She knew, even in that moment of passion, that if she scratched him, he'd beat her . . .

Later he watched the top of her head as she worked his penis like it was an oversized stick of candy. She licked it up and down, making it good and wet before popping it between her full lips and sucking him. She caressed his pouch while she suckled him, making wet, slurping noises because she knew he liked to hear them. He'd told her more than once that a woman who was enjoying what she was doing was noisy about it.

She continued to work on his penis, letting it spring free once in a while, slick and shiny with her saliva, then taking it back and sucking vigorously.

When she had it good and slippery wet she looked at him and, when he nodded, she turned and got on all fours. He knelt behind her, using the tip of his rod to probe for her wet opening, and then punched it home . . .

•   •   •

Satiated, he rolled off her and put his feet on the hardwood floor. He grabbed the makings from the table near the bed and constructed himself a cigarette.

"Was it okay?" she asked.

"Yeah, it was fine," he said to her.

She breathed a sigh of relief. This was the last night he was to be in town, if he had told her the truth. She'd wanted to satisfy him tonight and get away from him, hoping that she'd never have to see him again.

She was a whore, and she knew she wasn't supposed to climax when she was with one of her "men friends," but one of the other girls told her that she did with him *because* she was afraid of him.

"Aren't you afraid of him?" she asked her girlfriend.

"Sure, but he never asks for me. He asks for you, Lorene."

"I know," Lorene said, but now that it was over and this was his last night—and she'd satisfied him— maybe she'd get away from him without getting hit again.

Of course, she had complained to Madame Lisa that he hit her, but she was just as afraid of him as everyone else was—even the sheriff.

The people of Zenith, Colorado, were just waiting for Johnny Robak to leave town, so they could go back to living a more leisurely, less stressful life.

She watched as Robak rose and pulled his pants on, the cigarette dangling from his lip, his eyes narrowed against the rising smoke. Her heart was beating fast because she was afraid he was going to turn around and slap her just one more time before he left.

Please, God, she said, let him leave . . .

• • •

Robak finished belting his pants and slid into his shirt. He turned and looked at Lorene, who was sitting up in bed with all of her long blond hair hanging over one shoulder. He was almost sorry that he'd had to belt her around some, but that was what a woman needed to stay in line.

He sat on the bed to put his boots on and felt her flinch. When he finished with his boots he stood up and strapped on his gun—which was the real thing that everyone feared. They had all seen what Johnny Robak's gun could do. He was not yet thirty, but Robak felt sure he had the fastest gun in the West.

Fully dressed, Robak walked to the dresser and put some money on it. He then walked out of the room without looking at her or speaking to her.

He knew that would thrill her.

Robak had held Zenith under his thumb for the better part of a month and was only leaving his cushy existence here because he had heard the Gunsmith was in Colorado. All Robak needed to cement his place in history as the fastest gun who ever lived was a victory over Clint Adams, who had certainly been acknowledged as the fastest gun since Hickok's death.

Robak was going to change all that. He was going to kill Adams in a fair fight and walk off with his reputation.

Without his reputation Adams would be better off dead, anyway. Robak knew he felt that way, himself.

He stopped downstairs in the sitting room of the whorehouse to see if his partner, Jack Miller, was there. When he saw that he wasn't, he assumed Miller was still upstairs with the big-assed brunette he liked. He left the whorehouse, confident that Miller would be ready to leave in the morning.

Robak went back to his hotel early. He wanted to be up at first light and get started on his search for Clint Adams.

ONE

Clint Adams rode into Newcombe's Flats, Colorado, looking for nothing but a few peaceful days. The Flats was a small town, with one saloon and one hotel, and it was just what he was looking for. He directed his rig down the main street until he came to the livery and then made arrangements to board his team; rig; and Duke, his big black gelding. That done, he took his saddlebags and rifle and walked over to the hotel.

"Good evening," the desk clerk greeted. He was a young man with slicked-down hair and fuzzy cheeks. "Can I help you, sir?"

"I'd like a room, please."

"Fine, fine," the clerk said. "Please sign the register."

Clint signed it and accepted his key from the young man, who turned the register around to read his name.

"You're Clint Adams?"

Clint felt his stomach drop.

"That's right."

"The Gunsmith?"

"Look," Clint said, taking out a couple of coins. "There are a couple of these in it for you per day if you can keep that to yourself."

"Every day that you're here?" the kid asked.

"That's right, as long as I never hear the name 'Gunsmith,' and nobody else does, either."

The kid stared at the coins, licking his lips, and then took them.

"Deal?" Clint asked.

"Deal."

Clint looked at the kid then and said, "If you disappoint me I won't be very happy."

"Oh, no, Mr. Adams, I won't disappoint you. You can count on me."

"I hope so."

Clint went up the stairs to his room, not very proud of himself for trying to first buy the clerk, and then frighten him into silence. Still, if he was going to get the rest he wanted he was going to have to keep a low profile. He wouldn't be able to do that if everyone knew he was the Gunsmith.

He dropped his gear in his room, then left the hotel to go over and check out the saloon. If it was possible to get up a poker game in this small town, he might even stay longer. Nothing relaxed Clint like a long poker game.

He entered the saloon and, in spite of the fact that it was approaching evening, there were only two customers there, one seated at a table and one standing at the bar.

Clint went to the bar and asked the bored-looking bartender, "Is your beer cold?"

"Coldest beer in town."

Clint appreciated the irony of that statement and said, "Bring me one."

As it turned out, the beer was cold, and quite good.

"When does it liven up in here?" he asked.

"You looking for girls or gambling?"

"Poker."

The bartender shrugged.

"Might be some players in late tonight. You gonna be staying in town long?"

"A few days," Clint said. "I guess that depends on how I like it."

"Not much to like, not much not to like. If you don't mind having nothing to do most of the time, you'll like it."

"That's what I'm here for," Clint said. "To do nothing, and play poker."

"You might like it here."

"Uh, what about the women?"

"We got one pro in town, if you're interested."

"Not in paying for it."

The bartender shrugged.

"We got some women in town, but that's between you and them."

Clint finished his beer and put the empty mug down.

"Another?"

"Maybe later," Clint said. "Where can I get a good meal?"

"Only one place. Café down the street. Ain't got no name on the front, so you'll have to look in the window to make sure you got the right place."

"I'll find it."

"They make a mean steak and onions and a good stew."

"Thanks."

As Clint was leaving the bartender said, "Hey, mister . . ."

"Yeah?"

"What business you in?"

"I'm a gunsmith."

"Yeah? Might be some work for you here."

"Just send them over to the hotel," Clint said. "Much obliged."

He left the saloon and walked down the street, realizing that the bartender hadn't told him which direction to go. He'd gone a block when he decided he must have gone the wrong way. He turned just in time to be run into by a little girl of about seven years old. She had blond hair worn in pigtails and a sprinkling of freckles on the bridge of her nose.

"Whoa, girl," he said, catching her before she could fall.

"I'm sorry, mister," she said politely. She showed him a shiny coin in her hand and said, "My Ma give me some money for some licorice."

"Well, if I had some money for licorice, I'd be in a hurry, too."

"I didn't hurt you, did I?"

"No, honey, you didn't hurt me. Before you go, though, could you tell me where the café is?"

"Sure can, mister," she said. "My Ma owns it, and she's a real good cook. All you have to do is walk past the saloon about a block."

"Well, thanks very much."

"My name's Amanda, and my Ma's name is Caroline. You tell her I sent you, okay?"

"I will." The girl started to run toward the general store and called out behind her, "She's a real good cook, and real pretty, too."

She'd have to be, Clint thought, to be the mother of such a pretty little girl.

TWO

Clint entered the café and found an immediate similarity to the saloon—there were only two customers, seated at separate tables, eating dinner.

A woman came out of a back door, drying her hands on an apron, and asked, "Can I help you?" She had to be the girl's mother because she had the same blond hair, and the same sprinkling of freckles across the bridge of her nose.

"Doesn't anyone in this town eat dinner?"

She laughed.

"Unfortunately for me a lot of them eat it at home. Can I interest you in dinner?"

"I think so. A sweet little girl told me you were a very good cook."

"That would be my daughter, Amanda. How did you meet each other?"

"We literally ran into each other while she was on her way to buy a licorice stick."

"I promised it to her if she helped me with some dishes. Would you like a table? Take your pick."

"How about that one," Clint said.

"It's so far away from the window," she said.

"That's all right," Clint said. In fact that was why he picked it.

She led him to the table and said, "Would you like to see a menu?"

"I don't think so. The bartender said you make a very good steak with onions?"

"That's Harve. He eats here all the time. How about some potatoes and biscuits with that?"

"Sounds fine."

"What else did Amanda tell you after almost knocking you over?"

"She told me her mother was very pretty," Clint said, "and she was right."

Amanda's mother laughed and said, "I'll get that steak going. How about some coffee while you're waiting?"

"Black and strong, please."

"Coming up."

He watched her walk back into the kitchen. She was not a beautiful woman, but she was very pretty, and seemed to have an abundance of energy and a very nice personality.

She brought him a pot of coffee and a cup and he drank half the pot while waiting for his food, not because it took that long but because it was that good.

When she brought him his dinner he said, "That's the

best coffee I've had in a long time."

"Wait until you taste this steak," she said proudly.

"You mean Amanda was right?"

"Uh, about my cooking, yes. Everything is here but the biscuits. I'll go and get them."

While Clint was eating his dinner, Amanda came back into the café.

"Didn't I tell you my Ma could cook?" she asked him.

"Amanda, don't bother the man while he's eating," her mother said, coming out of the kitchen.

"The man's name is Clint," Clint said to both of them, "and yes, Amanda, you were right on both counts."

Amanda smiled at Clint proudly.

Her mother laughed, shook her head, and said to Clint, "My name is Caroline Fleming."

"I told him your first name already," Amanda said. "Did you have your licorice stick?"

"Yes, ma'am."

"Then get into the kitchen. I have some more dishes."

"I'll see you later, Clint."

"Enjoy your dinner," Caroline Fleming said, and followed her daughter into the kitchen.

Clint did enjoy the dinner, but he would also have enjoyed talking to Caroline Fleming some more.

Maybe later.

After dinner Clint went back to the saloon for another beer and talked to the bartender for a little while. As it got later a few more customers drifted in, some from a nearby ranch.

"You might be able to get some of those fellas into a poker game," Harve said.

Clint studied the men, who were obviously ranch hands, and decided against it. They all knew each other, and it was too easy to get cheated by playing in a game where you were the only stranger.

"I think I'll skip it, Harve," Clint said.

"Another beer, then?"

"Sure, one more and then maybe I'll turn in early. I'm not as young as I used to be. Traveling is taking more out of me than it used to."

"Maybe you need to settle down someplace," Harve said, giving Clint another beer.

"Here?"

"Shit no, not here," Harve said. "This place is nowhere."

"Nowhere is probably where I should settle down," Clint said, "but I don't think I'm ready to do that just yet."

Harve looked at Clint, waiting for him to continue, but when he didn't, the bartender moved down the bar to serve another customer.

THREE

Johnny Robak rode into Newcombe's Flats, hoping that he had finally caught up with the Gunsmith. He'd been trailing the man for eight days now, and every town he had come to he had found himself closer and closer behind him.

It was early evening, still an hour or so before dusk, and when Robak reached the livery he told the livery-man he would be staying just overnight.

Robak had learned everything he could about the Gunsmith, so he told the liveryman he'd walk his horse in and unsaddle him himself. The reason for this was so that he could check out the other horses in the stable. He knew that the Gunsmith rode a huge black gelding, and when he saw the black in the rear stall, his heart rate quickened.

He was here!

The sonofabitch was here, in Newcombe's Flats!

Hastily he removed the saddle from his horse and then picked up his gear. On his way out he told the liveryman to take care of the horse.

When he checked into the hotel he took a good hard look at the register and saw the name he was looking for: Clint Adams.

There was no mistake, now.

The Gunsmith was here.

"Is that who I think it is?" he asked the clerk.

"Who's that?" the clerk asked, frowning.

"There," Robak said, pointing. "That says Clint Adams. Is that the Gunsmith?"

The clerk hesitated a moment. He had been warned not to tell anyone that the Gunsmith was here, but this man was simply asking a question. He wanted to know if *this* Clint Adams was the *same* Clint Adams. He couldn't see any reason not to answer the man's question. After all, he was a guest.

"Yessir, that's him."

"Well," Robak said, "isn't that interesting. Would he be in his room now?"

The clerk turned and looked for Clint Adams' key.

"No, sir. My guess is he's eating dinner somewhere."

"Now there's an idea that appeals to me," Robak said. "Where would the best place in town for dinner be?"

"That'd be the café down the block, sir. Miss Caroline runs it, and she's the best cook in town."

"Well, I'll just leave my gear in my room and mosey over there for some dinner. Oh, before I go," he added.

"Yessir?"

"If I should see the Gunsmith I'd like to be able to recognize him. What's he look like?"

He listened intently while the clerk described to him the man whom he would very shortly kill.

FOUR

Of course, Clint had no real intention of turning in so early, and once some of the men in the saloon had started a poker game of their own free will, he decided that playing with them was better than being bored.

He was happy to find that there were only two men in the game who seemed to be from the same ranch. According to Harve, the third player was a town merchant, while the fourth was a stranger like Clint.

The stranger had entered the saloon shortly after dark and had probably arrived in town after Clint. He'd gone to the bar for a beer, and then seated himself at a table alone. He did not seem to be the one who had initiated the game.

"You fellas mind a fifth hand?" Clint asked, approaching the table.

"Hell no," one of the ranch hands said. "Five makes for a better game, anyway. Pull up a chair."

"Thanks."

The first hour of the game went relatively evenly. Clint was up about twenty dollars, as the game was being played for relatively small stakes. The stranger seemed to be up by the same amount, while the other three players were down the aggregate amount.

During the second hour, luck and skill turned the game Clint's way. He was by far the better player in the game, and on top of that, he was getting the cards he needed to fill or improve his hands.

During the third hour, when he was winning almost every other hand, Clint started to suspect something. He watched each of the other players deal several times, and came to the conclusion that the stranger was a better player than he was letting on. In addition, he was dealing Clint winning hands.

What Clint couldn't know was why. Why would a man he didn't know from Adam be dealing him winning hands?

At the end of the third hour, he found out the answer to his question.

"That's it," the other stranger said, dropping the deck to the table instead of dealing.

"You done?" one of the ranch hands asked.

"I'm done being cheated."

"What?" the other ranch hand asked.

"I don't know if you boys know it or not, but this fella here has been cheating," the stranger said, indicating Clint with a nod of his head.

All three men turned their heads and looked at Clint.

"Is that true, fella?" the town merchant asked. "You been cheating us?"

"No, I haven't," Clint said.

Now the three heads turned to look at the man who had accused him.

"Doesn't it strike you strange the way he's been winning?" the stranger asked.

"Could be he's lucky," one of the ranch hands said.

"Nobody's that lucky."

Clint agreed. He *had* been lucky, but the stranger had added to his luck by dealing him winning hands whenever he dealt.

"He has been winning an awful lot," the other ranch hand said.

"What do you say to that, mister?" the town merchant asked. "Why you winning so much if you ain't cheating?"

Now Clint knew that the stranger had him. If he claimed that the stranger was dealing him winning hands, what possible reason could he give? It would sound like a poor attempt to explain away his own cheating.

Still, he had to try.

"That man has been dealing me winning hands," he said, knowing it sounded ridiculous.

"Why would he do that?" one of the ranch hands asked. "You fellas partners?"

"I never met him before," the stranger said. "If we were partners, why would I be speaking up?"

"Man's got a point," the merchant said. "On the other hand, you ain't," he said to Clint. "Why would he be dealing you winning hands?"

"So he could accuse me of cheating."

"Why?" the man asked again.

"That's what I'd like to know," Clint said, leaning forward. "Why?" he asked the stranger.

"I don't know what you're talking about, fella," the stranger said, "but I do know this." Now he leaned forward in his chair. "I hate cheaters worse than I hate horse thieves."

The other players at the table now hastily rose and moved away. Others in the saloon caught on to what was happening and the bartender hurried around from behind the bar, holding a shotgun.

"I don't want no gunplay in my place, boys," he shouted, brandishing the shotgun. "Take it outside."

"It's too dark outside," Johnny Robak said. "I'll meet you out there tomorrow morning, friend."

"Why you pushing for this, friend?" Clint asked.

"I know who you are, Adams," Robak said, "and I never thought the Gunsmith could be a cheater."

Now the whole room knew who he was, and a murmur went up among them.

"But who you are don't matter," the other man went on. "You're a cheater, and Johnny Robak hates cheaters. I aim to make you pay."

"There are other ways of handling this," Clint said, but the other man would have no part of it.

"I don't know of any other way," Robak said, rising. He started past Clint and as he passed him said in a low voice, "I wouldn't have it any other way."

Robak walked to the door, then turned and said, "First light, friend. Be on the street." And he walked out.

Now all the attention was focused on Clint, and he rose.

"Who's the sheriff of this town?" he asked Harve.

"Pete Leach."

Clint never heard of him.

"Where would I find him at this time of night?"

"Probably in his office."

"Which is where?"

"Down the street to the left a couple of blocks."

"Thanks."

"You gonna meet him in the street?" Harve asked.

Clint knew everyone in the room was waiting for the answer to that one.

He said, "Not if I can help it."

FIVE

Clint knocked on the door to the sheriff's office and entered. The man behind the desk watched him as he approached his desk. He was tall—Clint could see that even though the man was seated with very black hair that came to a widow's peak, a beak-like nose, and a thin slash of a mouth. He looked like a competent, no-nonsense man.

"Sheriff Leach?"

"That's right." He had a tin cup of coffee by his elbow and he picked it up and took a sip. "What can I do for you?"

"My name is Clint Adams."

Clint waited a beat to see how the man would react.

"So?" the sheriff said.

"Do you know who I am?"

"Sure. What kind of a lawman would I be if I didn't know who the Gunsmith was? Am I supposed to be impressed?"

"Hell no," Clint said. "Why should you be impressed if I'm not?"

Leach frowned at that, not sure how to react to the remark.

Finally he said, "You want a cup of coffee?"

"Sure, thanks."

Leach stood up and Clint could see that not only was he tall, but he was easily six and a half feet tall. He pulled over a chair while the sheriff was pouring the coffee and accepted the cup gratefully.

"What's on your mind, Adams?" Leach asked, seating himself again.

"Staying out of trouble."

"That's admirable. How can I help you do that?"

Briefly, Clint told the sheriff what had happened at the saloon.

"Were you cheating?"

"No," Clint said, understanding why Leach had to ask that question. "I was having a run of luck, which was increased by the fact that this fella Robak was feeding me cards."

"Why would he do that?"

"So he could challenge me."

"You mean he set you up as a cheater so he could call you out into the street?"

"Right."

"Can you prove it?"

"No."

"In fact, the other players in the game would probably side with him, wouldn't they?"

"I'm sure ," Clint said. "My story sounded pretty thin even to me."

"And you think Robak was smart enough to set that up."

Clint looked at the sheriff.

"If he wasn't, that would mean I was cheating."

Leach held up both hands and said, "Hey, I'm just talking, Adams, I don't know either of you, do I?"

Grudgingly Clint said, "No, you don't."

"So all I've got is your word for all of this."

Clint nodded.

"What is it you want me to do?"

"I want you to keep this fella Robak from making me kill him."

"You're that confident, huh?"

Clint just gave the sheriff a tired look. It was a look that was born of a hundred Robaks who thought they were faster than the Gunsmith.

"I mean, it is possible that he could be faster, isn't it?" Leach asked.

"You'd like to find out, wouldn't you?" Clint asked, standing up.

"Look at it my way, Adams. Maybe you're just not sure you can beat this fella, and you want me to save your bacon for you."

Clint didn't know what to say to the man. He was asking for help to keep a man from being killed, and the sheriff was just too curious about the outcome to help.

"Forget it, Sheriff. I'll take care of it myself."

"I mean, what do you want me to do, throw the man in jail because he accused you of cheating? I can't throw every man into jail who . . ."

The rest of the sheriff's sentence was lost as Clint closed the door to the office behind him.

• • •

From his hotel room overlooking the street, Johnny Robak watched Clint Adams walk back to the hotel from the sheriff's office. Robak knew he had nothing to fear from the sheriff. He hadn't done anything illegal, but he found it real interesting that Adams had gone to the sheriff for help. That could only mean one thing.

Clint Adams had heard of Johnny Robak, and didn't think he could beat him.

Suddenly Robak felt ten feet tall and invincible. He wished he could go out into the street now and gun Adams down, but it would be better to wait until morning. It would be light, and there would be more people around to witness him outdrawing the Gunsmith.

And he definitely needed witnesses.

•

Caroline Fleming had heard from a couple of her customers, just before closing, about the proposed shootout between Clint Adams and a stranger who had accused him of cheating at cards.

She didn't believe what she'd heard. The man she had met, the one who had been so sweet to Amanda, could not be the kind of man who cheated at cards—even if he was the Gunsmith.

As for his reputation, she only had rumors and innuendo to go on, there. That's all that a man's reputation was. Again, she could only judge the man by what she had seen, and she had certainly not seen a killer or a cheat.

Caroline was worried about Amanda. Clint Adams had been all she talked about since she'd met him earlier that day, and now she knew about the shootout the next day. Caroline was going to have to do whatever she could to keep Amanda inside.

No matter what happened, no matter who was killed, she didn't want Amanda to see it.

Amanda Fleming pulled her sheet up to her neck and thought about Clint Adams. She knew her mother wouldn't let her out in the morning, so she was going to have to wake up extra early and sneak out before it even got light.

She wanted to see her friend Clint shoot that nasty man who called him a cheater.

When he reached his hotel room, Clint briefly considered going to Robak's room and trying to reason with him, but he decided not to. The man did not seem like someone you could reason with. He had his mind set, and that was that.

There were several ways Clint could go on this. First, he could mount up and ride out at first light, but that would accomplish nothing. A man like Robak would simply follow him and try again in the next town.

The other way was to simply refuse to meet the man, but that would have the same effect as the first way. The man would just keep trying. Also, if Clint left or refused, word would get around that he had lost it, that he was afraid. All that would do was to bring more Johnny Robaks out of the woodwork.

The third and final way was to go ahead and meet the man, and kill him. There was absolutely no way you could face a man with a gun, who was intent on killing you, and plan to wound him. If Clint faced Robak, he'd have to kill him or be killed, himself.

Reclining fully dressed on his bed, Clint looked at the ceiling and said, "What a way to live."

SIX

Clint was up before first light. He washed his face, using the pitcher and bowl on the dresser, and then checked his gun to make sure it was in proper working order.

After that he went to the window and waited.

Johnny Robak was awake before first light. He sat in a chair by the window, holding a gun in his hand, waiting.

At eight A.M. Clint decided to check and see if Caroline Fleming's café opened that early for breakfast.

From his window Robak could see Clint Adams walking down the street. He suspected that the Gunsmith was going in search of breakfast. He decided to let

him. He might as well have a decent, if not good, meal
before he died.

To his surprise, Clint found the café open. He stepped
inside and saw that he was the only one present. Caroline Fleming came out of the kitchen and stopped when
she saw him.

"Good morning," she said.

"Are you open for breakfast?"

"Of course. Have a seat. I'll bring you some coffee."

"Thank you."

Clint took the table farthest from the window. When
Caroline came out with the coffee, she didn't see him at
first, then she brought the coffee over to his table.

"Where is Amanda this morning?" Clint asked.

"Upstairs, still asleep."

"That's good."

"Eggs and potatoes?" she asked.

"Sure."

"And some ham?"

"Fine."

She started away, heading for the kitchen; then
stopped short and came back. She sat across from him
with a worried look on her face.

"Are you going to face that man this morning?"

He poured himself a cup of coffee before answering.

"If he gives me no other choice."

"Can't you make your own other choice?"

He smiled at her and said, "I've tried that in the past,
Caroline. It never works."

"You could leave town."

"He'd follow me."

"Perhaps not."

"Even if he didn't, word would get around that I ran
from a fight. Then there would be others. By taking care

of this problem, I avoid seven others."

She frowned and said, "It worries me that I can see the logic in that."

"Don't let it. How about that breakfast?"

"Right away."

Clint had gone over it a thousand times in his mind and unless Robak himself decided to give it up, he saw no way out but to face him.

He was starting his second cup of coffee when Caroline came out with his breakfast.

"It looks and smells delicious," he said as she put it down in front of him.

"Do you mind if I sit with you while you eat?" she asked.

"Why would I mind? It's not as if I'd be taking you away from your other customers."

"I'm afraid most of the people in this town who rise early make their own breakfast."

"Then why open this early?"

She lowered her eyes for a moment, then raised her chin, a bit defiantly.

"I opened hoping you'd come by for breakfast."

"And here I am. What do you think about that?"

"Clint... isn't there some way of avoiding this... this confrontation?"

"I wish there were, Caroline. I spoke to Sheriff Leach last night—"

"Him! I'm sure he wasn't much help."

"No, he wasn't."

"He's not much of a sheriff."

"He looks competent enough."

"He used to be, but he's grown complacent."

"That happens sometimes, when a man is in a job a long time."

"It wouldn't happen with you," she said.

He laughed.

"Oh, Caroline, it did. I was a lawman for a long time, and then . . ."

"And then what?"

"I gave it up."

"Not because you grew lazy."

"No."

"You don't want to kill that man, do you?"

Her breakfast was delicious, but he was fast losing his appetite. He put his utensils down with a louder bang than he'd intended.

"No, I do not want to kill that man!"

"Then why do it?"

"Because if I don't, he'll kill me. Now you must see the logic in *that!*"

She hesitated a moment, then said, "Yes, I'm sorry to say that I do."

Robak decided that Adams had had long enough to enjoy his breakfast. He was going to enjoy his, too.

After he killed the Gunsmith.

"Clint Adams!"

Caroline Fleming reacted sharply to the sound of Johnny Robak's voice. Her head turned so sharply she should have sprained her neck.

"Adams!" Robak called. "I'm waiting."

She looked at Clint.

"Are you going out?"

Clint picked up his fork again and said, "After I've finished my breakfast."

"You're going to eat before killing a man?"

He looked at her and said, "Or I'm going to eat before being killed."

SEVEN

Amanda Fleming had climbed out of her bedroom window and shinnied down a tree just before first light and, while her mother thought she was still asleep, she was sitting on the ground behind the café, with her back against the wall.

Where she had fallen asleep.

When Johnny Robak shouted, "Clint Adams!" Amanda came immediately awake. She got to her feet, sneaked around the side of the building, and peeked out into the street, where she saw Johnny Robak standing.

"Adams!" the bad man shouted again, and Amanda waited for the commotion to start. When it did, she was going to go out and tell Clint that she was on his side.

He'd like that.

"I'll go out and talk to him," Caroline said, standing up.

"Don't do that, Caroline."

"Why not?"

Again he slammed down his utensils.

"It will serve no purpose, except to make me a bigger target if word got around that I hid behind a woman's skirt!"

"You're worried about your reputation?"

Clint shook his head.

"You don't understand," he said. "Any sign of weakness on my part makes me a target for every two-bit hardcase who thinks he's good with a gun. By taking care of the problems I have to take care of, I avoid more. I thought you understood that."

"I guess I do."

She walked to the door and looked out the window.

"My God," she said.

"What?"

"There's a crowd gathering."

"I'm not surprised," he said. He had not picked up his fork again.

"It's . . . barbaric."

"That it is."

"Adams, I'm waiting for you!" Robak shouted. "Johnny Robak is waiting for you."

Caroline looked at Clint, who finally gave up on his breakfast and stood up.

He walked to the window and stood next to Caroline. Sure enough, the townspeople had come out for the show, lining both sides of the street.

"Caroline, make sure Amanda stays inside."

She looked up at him and said, "I will."

Clint looked out again at the crowd and said, "Yep, it's show time."

EIGHT

Clint stepped out of the café and saw Robak waiting for him in the street in front of the place. At the sight of him, Robak started walking to his right.

"There's still time to call this off, Robak," he called out.

"No way, Adams," Robak replied. "I've waited too long for this."

Adams figured that the younger man didn't mean that he'd been waiting a long time for Clint Adams, but for someone *like* Clint Adams.

If there was some way Clint Adams could give Robak his reputation, without anyone getting hurt, he would have. Let Johnny Robak see what it was like to be a hunted man—not hunted by the law, but by the "Johnny Robaks" of this world.

The two men continued to walk until they were standing facing each other in the street, which was lined on both sides by spectators. Clint had never been able to explain that. Not only was it morbid to be looking out for blood—like a crowd at a hanging—but there was always the chance of a stray bullet hitting an innocent bystander.

Well, at least little Amanda was upstairs in bed.

Amanda moved away from the café and into the crowd on her side of the street. She wanted to get a real good spot to watch the action, and to let Clint know she was there.

Caroline Fleming felt as if her heart was in her throat as she stared at Amanda's empty bed.

She turned and hurried downstairs.

Robak and Adams stared at each other. Neither man spoke, but neither man had to. They were watching each other closely, not waiting for someone to shout, "Go," but simply waiting for the other to make his move.

Finally Robak became the impatient one and his hand streaked for his gun.

Amanda Fleming chose that moment to run into the street to profess her support for Clint Adams.

"Clint! Wait!"

The voice belonged to a panic stricken Caroline Fleming who, as she exited her café, saw Amanda break from the crowd and run out into the street, directly between the two combatants.

• • •

Clint heard Caroline's voice, saw Amanda peripherally as he continued to watch Johnny Robak make his move.

"Amanda!" he shouted.

He reached for his gun, but Amanda was standing directly between him and Robak now, as Robak brought up his gun.

"Jesus," Clint thought, and then Robak fired . . .

Caroline screamed . . .

Clint knew he heard a scream, probably Caroline's, but his eyes were on Amanda.

He knew Robak had fired and he had not, and his eyes were on Amanda. He was waiting to see if a bullet was going to strike her, and when she didn't fall, he suddenly became aware of a burning sensation in his chest.

Everything around him seemed to be happening in slow motion. Robak still had his gun out, but he was not firing again . . .

People on both sides of the street were staring, or shouting, or covering their mouths . . .

He saw Sheriff Leach, who seemed to be watching the proceedings with a lot of interest . . .

Amanda was standing still, obviously frightened by the sound of the shot, and by her mother's scream . . .

Caroline Fleming had both hands pressed to her mouth and her eyes were wide as she stared at Clint Adams, watching the blood blossom on his chest like a rapidly blooming red rose . . .

Jesus, Clint thought, I'm shot.

The bastard shot me.

• • •

Everyone watching the proceedings had the same thought in their minds.

They were thinking nothing at all about Amanda Fleming.

All they were thinking was that they had seen history made this day.

The Gunsmith had been outdrawn!

NINE

Leach stepped into the street and walked to the fallen Gunsmith.

Caroline Fleming ran into the street and grabbed Amanda, kneeling down by her and hugging her tightly. Over her head she watched as Johnny Robak walked down the street toward them, and then past them as he approached the fallen figure of Clint Adams. She wanted to walk over to Clint also, but she didn't want Amanda to see him like that.

"Mama?"

"Yes, dear?"

"Is Clint dead?"

"I don't know, baby."

"Is it my fault?"

"No, baby, it's not your fault."

"Mama?"

"Yes?"

"Are you angry with me?"

Caroline looked at Amanda, kissed her on the forehead, and said, "Yes, dear, I'm very angry with you."

"Is he done?" Robak asked, holstering his gun. He saw Clint Adams' gun lying on the ground and leaned over to pick it up.

"Leave it," Leach said.

"What?"

"You shot the man. That entitles you to his reputation, but not to his personal belongings."

"Is he dead?"

Leach crouched over Adams, putting his hand on his chest next to the wound.

"I think so."

The crowds lining the street had now stepped into the street and were crowding around. Several of them darted foward and dipped handkerchiefs or portions of their clothing in the Gunsmith's blood, which was pooling in the dirt around him.

"All right, stand back now," Leach said, standing up. "Give the man some respect."

"Let me through," someone was saying, "let me through here . . ."

Presently a man broke through the crowd, carrying a black leather bag.

"Doc," Leach said, "I think he's dead."

"Where did you get your medical degree, Leach?" the man said.

Doctor Henry Ransom knelt down beside Clint Adams and began to examine the man. Ransom was a man in his mid-fifties. Craggy-faced and gruff-toned, he had no liking for most of the people in the town of Newcombe's Flats, and that included Sheriff Leach.

As a matter of fact, Ransom disliked most people, period.

"Should I send for the undertaker?" Leach asked.

Ransom scowled up at the sheriff and said, "Get me four men who won't drop him to carry this man to my office."

"He's not dead?" Robak asked.

"No, he's not dead, no thanks to you, I guess." At that moment a boy about fifteen leaned over and dipped his shirttail into the Gunsmith's blood.

"Can you get these people out of here!" Ransom shouted at Leach.

"All right, folks, let's move out of here. I need four men to carry Adams to Doc's office."

"I'll help," Robak said.

"You?" Leach said. "You want to finish the job?"

"The job's finished," Johnny Robak said. "I got what I wanted."

"Then I suggest you be on your way."

"I'll be leaving soon—"

"Now," Leach said. "Leave now."

Robak looked down at Clint Adams, then shrugged, and turned to push his way through the crowd. Part of the way through he suddenly encountered a woman and her child, still locked in their embrace.

"Are you happy now?" the woman asked him, giving him a withering look.

"Ma'am," he said honestly, "I've never been happier in my whole life."

TEN

Clint seemed to recall that he had awakened several times before, but he could not actually *remember* having done so. This time, however, he thought he would remember.

He was lying in a bed, staring up at the ceiling, and there was a dull ache in his chest. Slowly—so they wouldn't fall out—he moved his eyes away from the ceiling and saw the woman sitting next to him.

"Caroline?" he said.

She looked at him with concern and said, "Are you really awake this time?"

"I remembered you, didn't I?"

"You did the other times, too."

"How many other times?"

"Five."

"How long . . ." he began, but then his voice failed him.

"It's been three days."

"And I've awakened five times?"

"This makes six," she said. She peered at him intently and said, "You seem more alert, this time."

"Were you here all five times?"

"Yes."

"Why?"

"I was worried about you."

"How am I?"

"Alive."

"How bad . . ." he said, but his voice failed him again.

"You're weak," she said. "Don't try to talk too much."

He cleared his throat and said, "How bad was I hit?"

"Pretty bad. The doctor said the bullet missed your heart by an inch."

"Did he get it out?"

"Yes, but he said it wasn't easy."

"That's so he can raise his fee."

"I don't think—" she said, then stopped. "Well, at least you can joke."

"That's only because I'm not entirely sure what happened."

"You were shot, by Johnny Robak."

"He outdrew me?"

"He shot you," Caroline said, "that doesn't necessarily mean he outdrew you."

Suddenly Clint remembered.

"Amanda!" he said. "How's Amanda? Was she hurt?"

She put her hand on his shoulder to calm him.

"Take it easy. Amanda is fine. She wasn't hurt."

"Thank God," he said, relaxing.

"She blames herself, though."

"For what?"

"For getting you shot, almost getting killed."

"That's nonsense," he said. "I'm to blame for this."

"How can that be?"

"I picked up a gun, didn't I? Years ago? I've been headed for this for a long time," he said. "I'm lucky to be alive."

"But . . . you weren't outdrawn fairly. You stopped because of Amanda."

"That doesn't matter."

"But it does," she said. "It's not fair. Even the newspapers—"

"What about the newspapers?"

"I wasn't supposed to mention that to you," she said. "The doctor doesn't want you getting all worked up."

"I won't tell him if you won't," Clint said. "What about the newspapers?"

"They don't make any mention of Amanda," she explained. "All they say is that the legendary Gunsmith was finally outdrawn."

"Which is true."

"Not entirely—"

"Now who's getting worked up?"

"It's just not fair," she said. "A man of your reputation—"

"Reputation," he repeated. "Where's Robak?"

"He left town the same day. I was surprised that the sheriff made him do that."

"Leach," Clint said, as if testing his memory.

"That's right. He also wouldn't let Robak take your gun."

"My gun," Clint said, looking around.

"The sheriff has it in his office."

Clint frowned, thinking hard. Robak had outdrawn

him. The circumstances didn't matter, didn't alter that fact. That meant that when Robak left, he took Clint's "Gunsmith" reputation with him.

Clint Adams had always wondered how he could get rid of the reputation without getting killed.

Maybe this was it.

Maybe he was finally free.

He was brought back from his reverie by the arrival of a man with a black bag.

"Doctor," Caroline said. "He's awake and alert."

"Awake, eh?" the doctor said, approaching the bed. "How are you feeling, fella?"

"My chest aches."

"I don't wonder," the doctor said. "Let me have a look."

He pulled the sheet down off Clint, then set about undoing the bandage.

Caroline averted her eyes and said, "Clint, this is Dr. Ransom."

"You're lucky I was in town and not out delivering a baby—or a calf—somewhere," Ransom said.

"I suppose so."

"That idiot Leach had you pronounced dead. Would have sent you to the undertaker if I hadn't come along."

"I'm grateful to you for saving my life, Doctor."

"That's my job, friend," Ransom said. "Nasty-looking wound."

Clint felt the cool breeze touch the wound and looked down at it. It was raw, red, and purple, and he looked away. He'd been shot before, but never this badly.

"I'll put a fresh bandage on it."

"How soon before I can be up and around, Doc?"

"Think about it in terms of weeks, Mr. Adams," Dr. Ransom said, applying a new bandage. "Maybe even months."

"Where am I right now?"

"In the hotel. Of course, you'll have to foot the bill for the room."

"Of course . . . and your fee."

"Eventually. Luckily you've got a volunteer nurse."

Clint looked at Caroline, who smiled.

"Can I have visitors?"

"That depends on how alert you stay."

Now that the doctor mentioned it, Clint did feel a bit sleepy at the moment.

"Who did you have in mind?" Ransom asked.

Clint looked at Caroline and said, "A little girl who should know that she is not to blame for anything."

Ransom looked at Caroline, who was in turn looking at Clint.

"An admirable intention," the doctor said, closing his bag. "I'll check in on you a little later."

"Thanks again, Doc."

"Sure."

Caroline walked the doctor to the door and closed it behind him.

She returned to the bed and Clint looked at her, trying to keep his eyes open without much success.

"You'd better get some sleep," she said.

"I will," he said. "Will you have Amanda come up and see me?"

"Of course."

"I want to tell her . . . tell her that I . . . don't . . . blame her . . ."

"I appreciate . . ." Caroline started, but Clint had drifted off to sleep, and she settled down to watch over him.

ELEVEN

When Clint awoke the next time, Caroline questioned him and was satisfied that he remembered everything they had spoken about the last time he woke up.

"Where's Amanda?" he asked.

"She's afraid to come up."

"Why?"

"She thinks you're going to yell at her."

"Did you tell her I wouldn't?"

"Yes, but she's still afraid. I didn't want to force her—"

"No, of course not," Clint said. "Uh, do you have any newspapers?"

"Yes, but—"

"Let me see them."

"Are you sure?"

"Yes."

She handed him a copy of the *Newcombe's Flats Star*. He took it with his right hand, but when he tried to reach for it with his left, he gasped and lowered his hand.

"Here, let me fold it so you can hold it with one hand and read it."

She folded it and handed it back, and he read the story of the author's eyewitness account of the downfall of the Gunsmith.

. . . Robak's hand moved more quickly than the naked eye could imagine. Even the legendary Gunsmith couldn't believe the other man's speed. He gaped as Robak completely outdrew him and shot him in the chest. Stunned and hurt, the Gunsmith tried to raise his gun, but he could not. Finally, he dropped his gun to his side and keeled over, and all witnesses concerned could have sworn that he was dead . . . and he might as well have been, for his legend was dead, and isn't that the same thing?

"Jesus, what drivel," Clint said, dropping the paper onto the bed.

"On other pages he has further eyewitness accounts. Some of the larger papers in the country have picked them up."

"It's gotten all over the country, by now."

"I have some telegraph messages for you, Clint. They came just during this last period of time that you were asleep."

"Who from?"

"Would you like me to read them—"

"Just tell me who they're from."

"One from Bat Masterson, one from Wyatt Earp,
another from a man named Rick Hartman . . . I never
heard of him, but I've heard of the others."

"They're all friends."

"Another from a woman named Beverly Press . . ."

"Also a friend."

"Would you like me to read them . . . ?"

"No," he said. "They're just condolences. I'll read
them later."

"There's concern in all of them, for your health, but
no condolences," she said. "That's just for the dead."

"Yeah, you're right," he said. "Would you send out
replies for me, Caroline? Just tell them I'm fine and that
I'll contact them all when I'm back on my feet."

"Of course. I'll take care of it for you."

"Thanks," he said. He became aware of a gnawing
sensation in his stomach. "Jesus, when did I eat last?"

"You've had some soup a couple of times . . ."

"I don't remember."

"That's not very flattering to my soup," she said,
scolding him.

"I'm sure it was delicious. How about some now?"

"I'll go downstairs and bring some up," she said,
rising.

"Talk to Amanda for me, will you? Tell her that
seeing her would make me feel a lot better."

She touched his hand and said. "You're a very nice
man, do you know that?"

"Of course I do," he said, and she laughed and left. He
tried to stay awake until she returned, but it was a losing
battle that he finally lost.

The next time Clint awoke he saw little Amanda
Fleming standing by his bed.

"Hi," she said.

"Hi," he said.

"I'm sorry."

"For what, honey?"

"For getting you shot."

"You didn't shoot me."

"But you got shot because of me."

"That's a silly thing to say."

"Why?"

"Because it's not true."

She looked at her mother, who was standing nearby, and then back at Clint. She bit her lip, thinking about what she wanted to say.

"You could have beat that man if I wasn't in your way."

"There's no way to know that, Amanda. The only person to blame for me getting shot is me."

"You didn't do anything wrong, that other man did."

"Well, it's a little hard to explain," Clint said, "but the important thing for you to know is that what happened is not your fault."

"It's not?"

"No."

"Really and truly?"

"Really and truly."

Now she smiled, a great, beaming smile, obviously relieved that she was not going to be yelled at.

"Will you get better soon, Clint?"

"Real soon, honey."

"Come on, Amanda," Caroline said, "Mr. Adams has to get some rest."

"Can I come and see you again, Clint?"

"Sure, honey. I'd like that."

Caroline walked Amanda to the door and let her out.

"Thank you, Clint," she said. "She was so worried that you'd die and it would be her fault."

"Well, I think we've fixed that."

"I sent out the telegraph messages you asked me to," Caroline said.

"Thank you."

"I have a couple of answers wishing you well and the others should come in shortly."

"There was no answer necessary, but it's nice to get them."

"How do you feel?"

He thought a moment, taking a deep breath, moving his head, trying his arms.

"Sore."

"And you'll be like that for a while." She paused a moment, then said, "You've been shot before, haven't you?"

"Why do you ask?"

"I, uh, saw some scars when the doctor was bandaging you."

"You peeked, huh?"

"I did not," she said, a hot flush rising into her face and coloring her cheeks.

"The answer is yes, I have been shot before, and I've been stabbed a couple of times. I've been punched, kicked, hit on the head, and slapped by a few women in my time."

"Oh, I can't believe that last one."

"That's because I'm lying here, helpless."

"And in remarkably good humor for a man who has not only been shot, but whose life is bound to change by it."

"For the better," he said.

"Really? How so?"

"I'm no longer the invincible Gunsmith, the man who couldn't be outdrawn. That title now belongs to Johnny Robak. He's the man that all the youngsters with a gun will be looking for now. He's the one who'll have to sit with his back to the walls, and keep an eye in the mirror when he's standing at a bar. He's the one who's going to have to beware of an ambush on the trail, or from a roof."

"Has that been what your life has been like?" she asked, in awe.

"Yes."

"My God," she said. "It actually sounds like getting shot was the best thing to ever happen to you."

"Not always," he said, "but this time, yes, it looks that way."

TWELVE

It had been two weeks since Johnny Robak had shot the Gunsmith, Clint Adams.

Not only had he shot him, but he outdrew him.

It had taken a few days for the news to get out, and it wasn't until about four days later that Robak had ridden into a town and been recognized.

That town had been in Colorado, and since then he had ridden through New Mexico at a leisurely pace.

Now he was in Kelton, New Mexico, and everyone there knew who he was and what he had done

It was almost the same situation he'd had in Zenith, only here they were so respectful—and afraid—of him that they had virtually begged him to take the run of the town.

He was able to walk into any store and take whatever he wanted, and they told him not to worry about paying.

He was able to walk into the local whorehouse and take the whore of his choice, without paying.

Robak had been in Kelton for four days now, and he was tired of the whorehouse. He had seen a woman in town who interested him, only she was married. He was curious as to whether or not he'd be able to take her without having to kill her husband.

He decided to try it and see.

The woman worked in the general store with her husband and was usually behind the counter while her husband was helping people get their goods off the shelf, or she was working in a back storeroom.

Robak walked into the general store and the woman behind the counter stiffened. Her name was Lori Jeltz, and she had seen the way Robak looked at her the other times he'd been in the store.

Lori was thirty-one and a handsome, full-breasted woman with dark skin and dark hair. Her husband, on the other hand, was fifteen years older than she, and an inch shorter. She had married him because she felt safe with him, and at that time in her life—ten years ago— she'd needed to feel safe.

Robak stood in the doorway and stared at her. Dick Jeltz was in the storeroom, and she knew he would be there for some time. She returned Robak's look, and found herself breathing harder.

"Mrs. Jeltz?" The speaker was an older woman who Lori had been waiting on. "Mrs. Jeltz, that's all I need."

"Oh, I'm sorry, Mrs. Taylor. That'll be two dollars."

The older woman gave Lori Jeltz the two dollars, then turned and saw Robak.

"Hmph," she said, stepping past him. It was all the disapproval she had the nerve to display.

Now the store was empty, except for Lori and Robak.

"Hello," Robak said, approaching the counter.

"Hello, Mr. Robak," she said. "Is there something you need that you didn't get on your other visits?"

"Yes."

"What?"

"You."

She frowned and said, "I beg your pardon?"

"I want you, Mrs. . . . Jeltz, is it?"

"Yes."

"What's your first name?"

"Lori."

"Well, Lori, everything I've had in this town so far has been free, including the women. Are you free?"

"I'm married, Mr. Robak."

"That's not what I asked you."

"I'm sure there are plenty of women at Miss Millie's—"

"I don't want them," he said. "None of them excite me the way you do."

Nervously Lori looked at the curtained doorway that led to the storeroom.

"Is your husband back there?"

"Yes," she said. "He'll be out any moment."

"No he won't," Robak said. "He's probably back there taking inventory, isn't he?"

She hesitated a moment, then said, "Yes."

"And he'll be back there for some time, won't he?"

"Yes."

"Then I guess we'll have a lot of time together, won't we?"

She couldn't believe that he meant to . . . not right here, with her husband in the back room.

He wouldn't . . . would he?

THIRTEEN

"And you're as excited by me as I am by you, aren't you?"

She didn't answer.

"Aren't you?" he said, leaning over the counter closer to her. She backed away and bumped into a shelf.

"Y–yes," she said, because she was sure that was what he wanted to hear. Also, she felt excited—and was repulsed by the sensation. Sex with her husband had been pedestrian at best since the beginning, and had not gotten better the older he got. At times, when he wasn't around, she had taken to using her own fingers to achieve her pleasure.

Robak moved away from the counter and walked toward the door. For a moment she thought he was going to leave, but instead he closed the door and turned the CLOSED sign around so it faced the outside.

He turned and started walking back to the counter then, and she licked her full lips nervously. Her dark hair was pinned up over her head, and the first thing Robak did was unpin it so it tumbled down around her shoulders.

"You're beautiful," he said.

"Please . . ."

"I want you."

"No . . ."

"Right now."

"My husband!"

He smiled at her and reached for her shirt buttons.

"If he comes out . . ." he said, undoing the first button, "I'll have to kill him . . ." and he undid the second button.

"No . . ." she whispered, closing her eyes.

The smooth tops of her breasts came into view and he poked his finger between them. He was surprised that she wore no support. He didn't know that she enjoyed the way her shirt rubbed against her nipples during the day.

"If we're very quiet," he said, unbuttoning the next button, "he won't even hear us.

"Otherwise," he said, opening a fourth button and pulling the shirt free from her jeans, "I can go in the back and kill him now."

He waited for her now, standing there with her shirt hanging open. He could see most of her full breasts now, but he wanted to see more.

She was breathing hard, her breasts heaving, and finally she said, "A–all right."

He smiled and walked around the counter so he was on her side. He grasped her shirt and slid it slowly down her shoulders, letting it fall to the floor.

Her glorious breasts were naked now, and her nipples were rigid. She closed her eyes, embarrassed because she was excited by this man.

"I excite you," he said softly, touching his palms to her nipples, "because you know I've killed people." He closed his hand over her breasts, squeezing them, and she bit her lip. "I excite you because you know I shot the Gunsmith, beat him in a fair fight."

He kneaded her breasts, which were firm and warm in his hands, and said, "You're excited because you know I'm a legend, and because you're married to a man too old to satisfy you"

"God . . ." she whispered as he leaned over and, holding her breasts together, began to suck both nipples at the same time.

Her legs felt weak and she thought she was going to fall, but she didn't. She closed her eyes and surrendered herself to the sensations caused by his mouth and tongue and teeth . . . and then he released her and removed his mouth. The breeze touched her breasts, wet from his saliva, and chilled her.

He took her hands in his and moved them to his belt.

"Take down my pants," he said.

She undid the buckle, not looking. She didn't realize that he had taken off his gunbelt and put it on the counter. She finished undoing his pants and pushed them down his hips.

"All the way down," he said.

She pushed his pants all the way down his legs, and he left them there.

"Get on your knees."

She did.

"Pull down my shorts."

She did that, too, and suddenly his jutting erection

was right in front of her face. The scent that came from his crotch filled her nostrils and she breathed it in gently, savoring it. In all their years of marriage, she had never been this close to her husbands genitals.

"Take me in your mouth, Lori Jeltz," he said, putting his hands on her head. "Enjoy yourself, and make sure you do it quietly."

She didn't take him in her mouth immediately. Instead, she put her hand around him and ran it up and down, feeling the hardness and heat of him. With her other hand she hefted his balls. She'd dreamed about doing this with a man, but her husband would never let her. He said it was perverse.

The head of his penis was purple and swollen, and she leaned forward and swiped it with her tongue. Next she ran her tongue around it, still holding him with her hand. Finally she opened her mouth and allowed the spongy head to slide past her lips.

She moaned and he said, "Quiet," in a cautious tone.

She slid her mouth down the length of him, moving her hand out of the way, and then began bobbing her head up and down on him. He began moving his hips in unison with her head, and had to struggle to keep himself from moaning. This gal knew what to do with a man's penis!

She slid her mouth over him, wetting him, sucking him, reaching behind him and cupping his buttocks, squeezing him and sucking . . . sucking . . . sucking . . . and then he was coming in her mouth and for a moment she panicked. What should she do, she wondered, and then swallowed, and kept swallowing, never wondering where her husband was, never wondering what would happen if he walked out of the back room now . . .

Lori Jeltz, thirty-one, had her first taste of a man, and she loved it!

• • •

Robak pulled his pants back up and fastened them, and strapped on his gunbelt. Lori was still on the floor, sitting back on her haunches, dazed, unsure as to what had happened, licking her lips to clean them . . .

"Tonight," he said. "Come to my hotel room. Tonight. If you don't, your husband will never see another day."

"Yes," she said, and as he left, she thought that he needn't have threatened her.

She wanted to go to his room . . . desperately.

"I hate you," she said.

"I know."

"I'd kill you if I had the chance."

"There's the gun," he said, indicating it hanging on the bedpost, but she wasn't looking at it. She was sitting astride him, his erection buried deep inside of her, and she was talking as she bounced up and down on him.

"I loathe you," she said, bouncing, "Jesus, how you disgust me . . ."

"Just keep moving, baby," he told her, moving his hips, "keep moving . . ."

She had come to his room shortly after dark. He had no idea what she told her husband, but he didn't care. He told her to undress and she did. He told her to suck him, and she did. He told her to lie on the bed and spread her legs, and when she did that he mounted her and took her brutally. She moaned and gasped and clawed at his back and wrapped her legs around his hips, and when she came she would have screamed if she hadn't rolled her head to the side and taken a bite out of the pillow . . .

Now she was on top of him, this position her choice, and as she rode him she cursed him, threatened him, clawed at his chest, and when he exploded inside of her she struggled to keep her cries down and said through her teeth, "God, God, I hate you . . ."

She wasn't sure when she made the decision, but it must have been when Robak got down between her legs and began to lick her. No one had ever done that to her, and she had never even thought about it. In fact, she'd no idea what he was planning until his tongue touched her.

She jumped, thrilled by it, and then his tongue was probing her, sliding up into her, and then over her, up and down until he found her swollen little nub, and all of a sudden she was bouncing uncontrollably on the bed. Her orgasm was so intense that she thought she was going to die . . .

That must have been when she made her decision.

When Johnny Robak left Kelton, New Mexico, Lori Jeltz was going with him.

FOURTEEN

Three weeks after the bullet had violated his body, Clint Adams got up from bed.

Unfortunately, at that moment, Caroline Fleming, who had been at his side every day, walked into the room carrying a tray of food.

"Jesus Christ!" she said. "Are you crazy?"

"I'm sprouting roots in that damn bed."

"You're not supposed to be up."

"All I want to do is sit in a chair by the window," he said. "Maybe even open the window."

"Let me help you," she said, rushing forward.

"I can walk from the bed to the chair by myself," he said.

She watched as he walked slowly across the room to the chair and lowered himself into it.

"Are you proud of yourself?" she asked.

"Yes," he said. "Now how would you like to open the window for me?"

She put the tray down on the dresser and opened the window for him.

"Jesus, that feels good," he said as the breeze hit his face.

"How do you feel?"

As he did every time she asked him, he considered the question for a moment.

"Good," he said, finally, "I feel good."

"Still sore?"

"Not so much, now," he said. "It feels like somebody punched me in the chest."

"Is that an improvement?"

"Oh, sure," he said. "All this time it's been feeling like somebody was sticking a hot poker into my chest. This is much better." He looked at the tray of food and asked warily, "What did you bring me?"

"Solid food."

"Really?"

"The doctor said it's about time."

"I've been saying that for a week."

"I'll feed you—"

"Now look—"

"You look! I gave in and let you walk to the window. You want to put the tray on your lap and try cutting some meat?"

"No."

"Then let me feed you."

"All right."

She had brought him a piece of tender beef, some boiled potatoes and carrots.

"You cooked this, didn't you?" he asked around a piece of meat.

"Of course."

"I could tell."

"How?"

"It's delicious."

She smiled and gave him a potato.

"Where's my pard?"

"Amanda is in school."

"Is she coming up?"

"Yes, after school."

"Good."

"You really enjoy her visits, don't you?"

"Hers, and her mother's."

Caroline blushed and gave him a carrot.

"What will you do when you're able to travel?" she asked.

"I'm not going to think about that now," he said. "I'm a long way from being able to ride or to drive my rig."

She gave him another piece of meat.

He chewed, swallowed, and said, "How's Dukc?"

"He's fine. You ask me that every day. You love that horse, don't you?"

"Love's a strong word," he said. "I value his friendship."

"And he yours. Physically he's fine, but the liveryman says he just mopes around his stall every day."

"I'll have to go down and see him."

"Not today!" she said, firmly.

"No, not today," he agreed, "but soon."

"Clint."

"What?"

She gave him a potato.

"Amanda says she loves you."

"Really?"

"She wants to marry you when she grows up."

"By the time she's old enough to get married she won't want me. I'll be old and wrinkled, and I'll smell funny."

"Smell funny?"

"Old men smell funny. Didn't you ever notice that?"

"No, I never did," she said, laughing. She gave him some more meat and potatoes and carrots.

"Tell me something?" he asked.

"What?"

"How does Amanda's mother feel?"

Caroline hesitated, then said, "About what?"

"About me."

Another pause, and then she said without looking at him, "I want to help you."

"Out of guilt?"

"I suppose," she said.

"Some imagined guilt, I'd say."

"It was my daughter who rushed in front of you."

"I told you and her that that's nonsense. I want you to believe it."

"All right."

She gave him the last of the meal and then stood up.

"Let me help you back to bed."

He didn't argue. He stood and leaned on her and she brought him back to the bed.

"I'll see you a little later," she said, picking up the tray and starting for the door.

"Caroline?"

"Yes?" she said with her back to him.

"I don't want you to come back."

She hunched her shoulders, as if she'd been hit, and

then turned and looked at him.

"W—what?"

"I don't want you to come back later."

"Tomorrow?"

He shook his head.

"Not at all."

"B—but . . . why?"

"I don't want you to come back if it's out of guilt or pity," he said. "That's all."

She looked at him, something in her face changing. She'd been attractive, pretty even, but suddenly she was beautiful. She put the tray down, walked to the bed, and knelt next to it. She leaned over and kissed him.

It started as a gentle kiss, and then their lips melted together, fused by a need they both felt.

"It's not guilt," she said, "or pity."

She stood up, went to the dresser, retrieved the tray, and left.

Suddenly he felt a hundred times better.

FIFTEEN

A week later Clint was dressed and sitting in a straight-backed wooden chair on the boardwalk in front of the hotel. For the first time in his memory, he was not wearing his gun. It was upstairs in his room, in a drawer.

Caroline had walked down with him and left him in the chair, then had gone to take care of her lunch "crowd." Clint would wait there for her until she returned, and then go upstairs with her.

It was funny, but they had not talked about the kiss they'd shared a week ago. It was enough for him to know that she wasn't coming around out of pity or guilt. He suspected that she didn't know exactly what to call what she was feeling, but that was all right with him, because he was suffering from the same dilemma.

Clint looked up and saw Sheriff Leach crossing the street to approach him.

" 'Afternoon, Adams," Leach said.

"Sheriff."

"A month is a long time to spend in a hotel room."

"Too long," Clint said. "I would have come out sooner, but the doc wouldn't let me."

"And Mrs. Fleming?"

"What about her?"

"I suppose she wouldn't let you, either."

Clint studied the man, looking for some hidden meaning to the remark.

"She's been a good nurse."

Leach nodded.

"When do you think you'll be able to travel?"

"You should ask Doc that."

"I suppose I should."

"You in a hurry for me to leave?"

"Frankly . . . yes."

"Why is that?"

"I don't want any trouble here."

Clint laughed.

"That prospect didn't bother you a month ago."

"Maybe I handled that wrong," Leach said, "but I aim to handle this part right."

"Which part is that?"

"The part that gets you out of Newcombe's Flats before the tinhorns come looking for you."

"You got me wrong, Sheriff," Clint said. "I'm a peaceable man. The man you're thinking of died a month ago."

"You're still the Gunsmith."

"No, I'm not. I'm Clint Adams. I'm *a* gunsmith, but

I'm no longer *the* Gunsmith, and I can't say I miss the fella."

"You're not wearing your gun."

"No point," Clint said. "Wouldn't be able to use it even if I had to."

"Why's that?"

"The chest wound left both arms a little stiff."

"That permanent?"

Clint shrugged.

"The doc doesn't know. Says we have to wait and see."

"So you'll be around some longer, huh?"

"Some, Sheriff . . . but not looking for any trouble."

"What about Robak?"

"What about him?"

"You gonna let him get away with gunning you, with riding out with your rep?"

"My rep?" Clint said, laughing again. "It's his now, Sheriff, and he's welcome to it."

Leach stared at Clint for a few moments longer, not sure of what he was seeing, then executed a small wave and walked off. If some tinhorns came to town to see if they could trade some shots with the Gunsmith and come out on top like Johnny Robak did, he hoped that Adams wouldn't expect him to stand up to them for him.

"What did he want?"

Clint turned and saw Caroline. She was fresh from her kitchen and smelled of fried foods and baking dough, and she was sweaty and beautiful.

"Wanted to know when I was leaving town."

"Why?"

"I guess he's nervous."

"Didn't you tell him you can't use your gun?"

"I did."

"Maybe I should talk to him—"

"You going to fight my battles for me?" he asked. "Isn't that what you nursed me back to health for? So I'd be able to fight my own?"

"I don't want you to have to fight at all," she said. "Ever again."

He didn't know what to say to that, it was said with such intensity.

"Do you know what I realized while I was in my kitchen, frying chicken and baking bread?"

"What?" he asked, totally unprepared for what was to come.

"I love you."

He stared at her.

"Did you hear what I said, Clint Adams?" she said. "I love you."

"I–I heard you."

"Does that scare you?"

"To death."

She looked up at the sun, then said, "I think we'd better get you back to your room."

SIXTEEN

"It might not be love, you know," he said as she helped him into bed.

"Why not?"

"Well, patients usually fall in love with their doctors, or their nurses."

"And it never happens the other way around?" she asked, pulling off his boots.

"I guess it's possible," he said.

"Then why not this time?"

"Because . . ." he said.

She loosened his pants and pulled them off while he unbuttoned his shirt and removed it.

"Lie down," she said, putting her hand against his bare chest.

She'd touched him many times in the past weeks, but

this time there was something different in her touch. As he laid back she ran her hand over his stomach in small circles, just below the bandage that wrapped around his chest.

"Caroline . . ."

"Just keep quiet," she said. "I'm relaxing you."

He was anything but relaxed as her hand moved lower.

"Amanda . . ."

"Is in school," she said, leaning over and kissing his belly. Her lips moved on his skin and he felt his penis swell. She put her hand on him over his underwear, then slid her hand beneath his waistband and pulled it down so that the head of his penis was visible. She moved her mouth lower, over his navel, until she could lick the spongy head of his cock. He moaned and moved his hips, lifting off the bed, and she pulled his underwear down his legs and off.

"You were right, you know," she said, taking his rigid penis in her hand.

"About what?" he asked, breathlessly.

"When you said that I peeked at you."

She switched hands so that she held his penis in her right and then used her left to caress his testicles.

"I didn't just peek," she said, moving her lips up and down the length of him. "I stared . . . and I wanted you . . . Oh, I wanted you . . ." she said, and her lips swooped down over him and took him fully into her mouth.

Her head began to bob up and down as her mouth rode him and he reached down to tangle his fingers in her long, blond hair. He bit his lips as she sucked him and then suddenly he was coming, filling her mouth, and she sucked and swallowed, squeezing his thighs and moaning . . .

She stood up then, licking her lips, and asked. "Did it hurt?"

"It did," he said. "It was wonderful."

She laughed throatily and said, "I meant did it hurt your wound?"

"Oh, that . . . no, it didn't hurt."

"Well, then, maybe we can try something else . . ." and with that she began to undress for him.

She stripped off her clothes with confidence. Her breasts were large and firm, with light brown aureola that led to darker nipples. When she pulled her pants off he saw that her belly bore the marks of childbirth, but that only made her even more desirable to him. Her thighs were smooth and a touch too full, her calves strong and hard from all the walking she had to do all day.

"You're beautiful," he said as she joined him on the bed.

"You tell me when it hurts," she said, reaching for his semierect penis again. She pressed her body against him and the heat of her was intense. Immediately—amazingly—his penis began to swell again.

She kissed him, her tongue sliding into his mouth. He wanted to reach for her, but as he did he felt a twinge in his chest, which she sensed.

"Easy," she said. "Just lie back and let me do everything."

"I want you . . ." he said.

"Let me do it," she said. "There will be other times, but now let me do it."

Finally he agreed and settled back and she began to use her mouth and her hands, bringing his body alive. When she had his penis standing rigidly she mounted him gently and eased herself down over him, swallowing him into her steaming womanhood.

She rode him easily, smiling at him, putting her hands against his stomach so she could take some of her weight off of him with her arms. He put his hands on her ribs, then slid them up to cup her breasts and flicked the nipples with his thumbs. Her breasts had deep, full undersides, her skin was smooth and hot as he hefted the weight of her breasts.

He felt her belly begin to tremble and she leaned her head back and gave herself up completely to the sensations of her climax. Moments later he exploded inside of her and they moaned together, aware of nothing in the world but each other . . .

Later, they were lying side by side, her head on his shoulder.

"Amanda should be coming home soon," he said.

"I know, and I'll have to open the café again."

"You must have lost a lot of business these past weeks, sitting up here with me with no one to keep it running for you," he said.

"The café is not such a great money maker, Clint."

"How do you live?"

"I have some savings, and as long as I'm open for lunch and dinner we do all right."

"What about when you're too tired to open or too sick?"

She laughed and said to him, "There's no such thing as being *too* tired, and when I'm sick, the café just has to stay closed."

"Maybe . . ." he said, "maybe what you need is some help."

"Oh sure," she said, "all I have to do is hire someone and hope they'll work for meat and potatoes."

"You don't have to hire someone," he said. "You have me."

"You?" She laughed and asked him, "Can you cook?"

"Hardtack and beans," he said, "but I can learn. And I could wait tables."

She picked her head up and stared at him.

"Are you serious?"

"Sure I am."

"You can't be."

"Why not?"

"Excuse me, Clint, but after the kind of life you've led, I can't see you waiting tables in a café."

"What about if I was part owner?"

She frowned and said, "What are you saying?"

"I'm saying I could buy into the café," he said. "We could fix it up a little—you know, get some new tables, new tablecloths . . ."

"Oh," she said, and he thought he detected some disappointment in her tone. Had she thought he was going to propose marriage? Had he even thought of that himself? He wasn't sure, but buying into the café was a way to start off slowly. After all, patients do fall in love with their nurses, and he had to be sure that this wasn't simply a case like that.

"I have to get dressed and go and meet Amanda," she said, sliding her legs from the bed to the floor.

"Will you think about my . . . my proposition?" he asked. He'd almost said "proposal."

Dressing quickly, she said, "I'll think about it, Clint, but I think you should think about it, too . . . seriously. We can talk about it again later."

"Will you be coming back for dinner?" he asked.

"I'll bring you dinner—"

"No, let me come to the café for dinner," he said.

She looked at him and said, "Do you feel up to it?"

"Definitely."

She looked at him for a few moments, then walked to the bed and kissed him gently.

"I'll come for you," she said. "See you later."

"All right."

When she left he laid there and stared at the ceiling. Was he in love with Caroline Fleming? He knew he loved her little girl, Amanda, but that was the kind of nonthreatening love he could admit to.

The other kind would take some time . . .

SEVENTEEN

Two weeks later the new tables were in, the new tablecloths were in, and Clint Adams was waiting tables in Caroline's Café . . .

They had talked about Clint's "proposition" several times during the ensuing two weeks, but Clint stood fast on his position. He wanted to stay in Newcombe's Flats for a while and learn the café business . . .

The afternoon before Clint started in the café he and Caroline went for a ride. It was the first time Clint had exercised Duke since the shooting.

"How do you feel?" Caroline asked, watching him with concern.

"I'm fine," he said, sitting up straight in the saddle. It

felt good to be on Duke's back again, and the big gelding obviously felt good stretching his legs, as well.

"Maybe we should go back," she suggested.

"No, I'm fine, really."

"Clint, let's talk about this decision of yours . . ."

"Our decision," Clint said, correcting her. "It takes two to make a partnership."

"All right," she said, "our decision. How long do you think this will last?"

"I don't know," he said.

"How long will it be before you get the itch to move on again?"

"I don't know the answer to that one, either, Caroline. Are you trying to force me to make a decision about that?"

"No, I'm not trying to force you into anything. I wouldn't want to force you into anything . . ."

"Well, that's good. Then let's just get the partnership underway and see what happens."

"All right."

"The new tables and tablecloths should be here by tomorrow."

"What?"

"I ordered them a few weeks ago, when we first talked about this."

"I can't pay—"

"I can. Also, I think the place needs a name."

"Like what?"

"Like 'Caroline's Café.' How do you like it?"

"I don't," she said, making a face.

"Well, I already ordered the sign."

"What?" she said, and he could see she was on the verge of getting angry.

Quickly he said, "It was either that, or 'Clint's Café.' "

She paused a moment, then nodded and said, " 'Caroline's' it is."

They laughed, and rode back to town . . .

It took Clint a while to learn to balance plates on his arms, and carry pitchers of water and beer without spilling any of it.

Luckily business did not improve immediately upon installation of the new tables and tablecloths and the new sign, and so Clint did not have cause to try his new balancing act with real customers.

"Well, the breakfast rush is over," he said to Caroline, watching while she prepared some soup for lunch.

"That's because nobody came," she said, giving him a look.

"Lunch will be better," he said, with assurance.

"I don't know," she said. "We've lost one customer already."

"Oh? Who?"

"You."

"That's right," Clint said brightly. "Owners eat free, don't we?"

"Yes, we do."

Clint heard someone enter the café and said, "Here comes the lunch crowd . . ."

"Watch for the stampede," Caroline called out.

Later, when Amanda came home from school, she followed Clint around, helped him wait tables, and talked to him incessantly.

He loved it.

"Amanda," Caroline said at one point, "you're going to talk Clint's ear off."

"He doesn't mind, do you Clint?"

"I don't mind at all, honey," he said, and went out to bring a pitcher of beer to a table.

"Mama?"

"Yes, honey?"

"Are you going to marry Clint?"

Caroline turned her head from the stove to look at her daughter.

"Why do you ask that, Amanda?"

"Because I love Clint, Mama, and I think you do, too."

"Well, that may be, Amanda," Caroline said, "but what about what Clint feels?"

"I know he loves me."

"Did he tell you that?"

"No, but I can tell, just like I can tell he loves you, too."

"You can tell, huh?"

"Yes. You do love him, don't you, Mama?"

Caroline stepped away from the stove and went down on one knee to hug her daughter.

"Yes, I do, Amanda. I love him, but as far as us getting married, that's going to be up to Clint."

"Why can't you ask him?"

Feeling a flush rise into her face, Caroline stood up and busied herself at the stove.

"It just doesn't work that way, Amanda."

"Why not?"

"It just doesn't. Hand me that fork . . ."

"Hey," Clint said, reentering the kitchen, "where's my helper?"

"I'm coming," Amanda said. "I was just talking to Mama about—"

"Amanda!"

Amanda laughed and went out into the dining area.

"Something I should know about?" Clint asked.

"No," Caroline said innocently, "just some mother/daughter stuff. What was that last order, again?"

EIGHTEEN

"Did you hear?" Deputy Jerry Paul asked Sheriff Pete Leach.

"Hear what?"

"The Gunsmith is waiting tables over at the café."

"What?" Leach asked, looking up from his desk. "Where did you hear that?"

"Heard it from Elmo Cook. He went over there for lunch and was waited on by the Gunsmith himself."

Leach thought that over for a moment.

"He's paying Caroline Fleming back, then, for nursing him back to health."

"I don't know," Jerry Paul said. "They got new tables, and new tablecloths, and a brand-new sign outside that says 'Caroline's Café'."

"Now where would she get the money for that?"

Leach asked. "Unless Adams gave it to her."

"Well, the way I hear," Paul said, "the Gunsmith has bought himself a piece of the café."

"He's a partner?" Leach said.

Paul shrugged and said, "That's what I heard."

"Jesus," Leach said, "maybe he's never gonna leave."

"Thing like that could put this town on the map," Jerry Paul said.

"Or wipe it off," Leach said, standing up.

"Where you going?"

"Out to lunch!"

"What are you trying to pull," Leach demanded when Clint came to his table.

"What do you mean?"

"I thought I made it clear that I wanted you to leave town."

"When I felt up to it."

"So?"

"So, I don't feel up to it. What'll you have? We've got some great soup."

"Look," Leach said, "I may not be the best lawman in the world, but I know one thing."

"What?"

"All you're gonna do for this town is bring trouble."

"I'm not even wearing a gun, Sheriff."

"That won't stop trouble."

"You worry too much. Try the soup?"

"Yeah," Leach said, "yeah, bring me the goddamn soup."

To the surprise of both Caroline and Clint, the dinner crowd was such that they had people waiting for tables.

Clint really got a workout waiting tables with only Amanda to help him, but by the time the last diner left, he felt pretty good about himself.

"Well, how did I do?" he asked Caroline, removing his apron.

She came out of the kitchen with a pot of coffee and poured them each a cup. Amanda had been sent to bed an hour earlier.

"You did fine, but . . ."

"But what?" he asked, sitting opposite her at one of the tables.

"Why were we so busy tonight?"

"Maybe the word got around about how good a cook you are," he said.

"Or maybe," she said, "word got around that the Gunsmith was waiting tables?"

He made a face and said, "That occurred to you, too, huh?"

"Yes. Clint, can we avoid trouble?"

"There was no trouble tonight, was there?" he asked.

"No, but—"

"Well, let's not worry about it until it comes, all right?" he said. "Let's not look for trouble where there is none."

"All right," she said. She smiled at him then and said, "You were really good tonight, you know?"

"I know," he said proudly. "I only broke one dish."

"Speaking of dishes . . ."

NINETEEN

Johnny Robak woke up six weeks after outdrawing the Gunsmith, and was unhappy.

Lying next to him in bed was Lori Jeltz, who was still with him. They were in a small Mexican town the name of which Robak couldn't pronounce.

He reached down to the floor on his side of the bed and found the whiskey bottle that was lying there. It still had a mouthful in it, and he tipped it up and drained it.

Things had not gone the way Johnny Robak had imagined they would. Of course, towns still showed him respect when they found out who he was and what he wanted, but that wasn't enough for him. It wasn't *real* respect, it was just fear. Also, his name had faded from the newspapers relatively quickly. His legend just was not growing the way he had expected it to.

Damn it, he'd outdrawn the Gunsmith, put a man down fair and square in the street, in front of witnesses. What more did they want?

He knew the answer to that one without anyone telling him.

He'd left Clint Adams alive, and people were holding that against him. His legend was not growing because the Gunsmith was still alive. Now, if he had *killed* the Gunsmith, then there would be no denying him his due.

What he had to do, then, was go back to Newcombe's Flats and finish the job.

Next to him Lori Jeltz stirred and rolled against him. Another thing he was going to have to do was get rid of Lori. She still had a marvelous body and she was delicious, but those things were available in every town he'd come to, without bringing them along with him. Also, Lori was starting to get a little too possessive and a bit too demanding. She wanted more from Johnny Robak than he was willing to give any woman—and that was aside from her sexual demands.

Now she reached behind her, slid her hand between his legs and grabbed hold of his penis. Immediately it started to swell in her hand.

He turned her over on her back and mounted her, sliding his penis brutally into her, cupping her buttocks with his big hands.

Might as well get some use out of her while she was still here.

Lori Jeltz closed her eyes and wrapped her legs around Johnny Robak's waist. She couldn't get enough of him and demanded sex at all times of the day, in bed or on the floor, or out on the trail. It had gotten so that she could not imagine ever being without him. All those years of passionless marriage had not prepared her for what real passion was like, and now she didn't ever want to be without it again.

Sure, he hit her once in a while, which was something else that her husband had never done to her, but she felt that as long as she kept him satisfied and kept her legs open for him, she wouldn't have to worry about his leaving her.

She found out later that she was wrong.

After Lori'd fallen asleep, Johnny Robak got up and got dressed.

"Good-bye, sweetie," he said. "It was fun while it lasted, but you'll only slow me down."

She was becoming a weight around his neck, in more ways than one.

He left a few bucks on the dresser top and left. He went right to the livery stable and saddled his horse.

After she got over the shock, she could always go back to her husband, but he couldn't worry about her. He had business to attend to.

He had killed the *legend,* but he had not killed the *man*.

He had to set that right.

TWENTY

As soon as they walked in, Clint sensed that trouble was coming. That instinct had not reared its head and bitten him for weeks, but it had not weakened from lack of use. It stood up on its hind legs now and bit him on the ass.

"Honey," he said to Amanda, "I think it's time for you to go to bed."

"But it's still early," she complained.

"Do as I say, Amanda."

She frowned and stared at him. He had never used that tone of voice on her before. He almost sounded like he was her father.

That made her smile.

"All right," she said. "I'll go and tell Mama good-night."

"All right."

The three men looked around, picked out a table, and

walked to it. On the way, they passed a man and a
woman who were leaving, and one of them deliberately
shoved the man so that he staggered off balance.

The three of them began to laugh and seated them-
selves at their table.

Clint dried his hands on his apron and walked over to
take their order.

"What'll be, gents?" he asked.

All three men looked up at him. They were all in their
thirties, wearing trail-worn clothes and the look of men
who think the world owes them something.

"What'll we have?" one of them asked the other two.
"You serve beer here, waiter?"

"We do."

"Then we'll start with a pitcher of beer—and make
it cold."

Clint nodded and went to get it.

"What did you do to Amanda?" Caroline asked as he
entered the kitchen.

"What do mean?" he asked, filling the pitcher from a
cold barrel.

"She went to bed early, and she had a smile on her
face."

"She's a good kid," he said. "I'll be right back."

He brought the pitcher of beer and three glasses to the
table and set them down.

"Naw, I think you're wrong, Dale," the man who had
ordered the beer said, speaking to one of his friends.

"I don't know, Kenny," the man called Dale said. "It
sure looks like him."

"Naw, it couldn't be," Kenny said. "What do you
think, Phil?"

The man named Phil simply shrugged and poured out
three glasses of beer.

"You fellas care to order something to eat?"

"Well, that's why we're here, ain't it?" Kenny asked. "What's good, waiter?"

"The beef stew is our specialty."

"Well then, we'll have three beef stews, won't we, fellas?"

Dale nodded his agreement, but Phil said, "I'll have a steak."

"You heard the man, waiter. Two stews and a steak."

"Coming up."

Clint went into the kitchen and gave Caroline the order.

"Is something wrong?" she asked, filling the two bowls with stew.

"No, why?"

"You sent Amanda to bed early, and we're still busy."

"I can handle it."

"Clint—" she began, but he was already out the door.

He put the two beef stews down in front of the men and they began to eat.

"I'll bring some bread with the steak."

He went into the kitchen to get the bread and steak, and was out before Caroline could stop him. She moved to the curtained doorway and pushed the curtain aside to watch him.

As Clint put the steak and bread on the table the men continued to eat, and he started to think that maybe he'd been wrong. As he started away, though, Kenny reached out and took hold of his wrist in a strong grip.

"Hey, waiter," Kenny said. "My friend here tells me you look like somebody he saw once."

"Who might that be?"

"Fella called the Gunsmith. Is that true?"

"My name's Clint Adams."

Kenny looked at Dale, who nodded with wide eyes.

"He says yup, that's you, the Gunsmith."

"So?"

"So he says you got beat a few weeks back, and here you are waiting tables. Is that true? Did somebody outdraw the legendary Gunsmith and drive you to waiting tables?"

Clint didn't answer.

Suddenly the man named Phil reached over and flicked Clint's apron away.

"He ain't even wearing a gun."

"Ooh," Kenny said, "waiting tables and not wearing a gun. I guess the story must be true."

"What's that mean to you?" Clint asked.

"Well, maybe I'd like to give you a try, Adams. Maybe I can outdraw the Gunsmith. What do you think of that?"

"I think you'd better let go of my wrist. I have other tables to take care of."

"Hear that, boys?" Kenny said, tightening his grip. "The man says he's got other tables to take care of. Hey, waiter, you still got this table to take care of. How about it? You and me out in the street."

"We don't serve out in the street," Clint said.

"Smart mouth—" Kenny said, but he was cut off as Clint suddenly turned his wrist clockwise, forcing Kenny's grip open.

"Eat your dinner, friend, and then get out."

"Hey, don't turn away from me—" Kenny said. He started to pull his gun out with his right hand; his left hand was flat on the table. Clint grabbed Phil's steak knife and brought it down hard, piercing Kenny's hand and pinning it to the table.

Kenny screamed, and Phil pulled his gun and shoved it underneath Clint's chin.

"Mister," Clint said to him, "you better do yourself a

favor and pull that trigger right now."

"He ain't got a gun, Phil," Dale said. "There's law in this town."

Kenny, whimpering, pulled the knife free with his right hand and threw it on the floor. He took a napkin and wrapped it around his wounded hand.

"Kenny?"

"Don't shoot, Phil," Kenny said, between his teeth. "He's mine." Kenny looked at Clint and said, "On the street tomorrow, *waiter,* or we'll burn this place to the ground."

The three men started to rise, Phil continuing to hold his gun beneath Clint's chin. When Kenny stood up he kicked his chair away and then swung his right hand viciously into Clint's mid-section. Clint grunted and fell down to one knee, and Phil pulled his gun away and holstered it.

"Tomorrow morning, Adams," Kenny said. "I'll be waiting for you."

As the three men left the café the other diners began to buzz, and Caroline came running from the kitchen and crouched next to Clint.

"Are you all right?"

He drew in a painful breath and said, "Yeah, yeah, I'm fine."

He had a piercing pain in his chest as well as the ache in his stomach, but he didn't mention that to her. Still, when she tried to bring him to his feet, he gasped at the pain and couldn't help clutching his chest.

"Somebody go for the doctor!" she cried out.

"Caroline—"

"Come on. We'll get you upstairs." She turned her head and shouted again, "Get the doctor!" and a man rose and ran from the café to do just that.

TWENTY-ONE

Clint was reclining on Caroline's bed with the doctor seated in a chair next to him. The ache in his stomach had subsided, but there was still a dull pain in his chest.

Caroline and Amanda were both standing in the doorway, watching. Amanda was holding tightly to her mother's waist, watching Clint with deep concern in her eyes.

"There shouldn't be any permanent damage," the doctor finally said. "The wound may be almost healed on the outside, but there's still got to be some trauma inside. The blow you received simply amplified it."

"Will he be all right?" Amanda asked.

The doctor turned and said, "Why aren't you in bed, little girl?"

"Is Clint gonna be all right?" she demanded again, more stridently.

"Yes, yes, he'll be fine," the doctor said. "All he needs is some rest."

The doctor closed his bag and stood up.

"And don't be doing anything else to mess up my brilliant work," he said to Clint. "Getting into fights . . ." the man muttered as he left.

Caroline walked the doctor out, while Amanda went to the bed and stared at Clint.

"Are you all right, Clint?"

"I'm fine, honey."

"Can I kiss you?"

"I'd love you to kiss me."

She leaned over and kissed him on the cheek.

"I heard what happened," she said. "You sent me to bed because you knew there would be trouble with those men, didn't you?"

"I had a feeling."

"Are you gonna do it?"

"Do what?"

"Meet that man in the street tomorrow?"

"Well, honey, that's hard to say—"

"He is not!" Caroline said, coming into the room. She put her hands on her daughter's shoulders and said, "Amanda, it's time for you to go to bed."

"Yes, Mama."

She walked to the door slowly, then turned quickly and said, "If you do face that man in the street, Clint, I'll stay out of the way this time. I promise!"

"Amanda!" Caroline said, but the little girl ran from the room and into her own.

Caroline walked to the bed, pushed aside the chair the doctor had used, and sat on it.

She put her hand on Clint's arm and said, "I thought that man was going to shoot you."

"He didn't have the nerve."

"You taunted him," she said, "as if you wanted him to shoot."

"I knew he wouldn't . . ."

She shook her head and said, "I don't understand that. You'll stay here tonight instead of going to your hotel."

"All right," he said, without choosing to argue, "but you'll have to do something for me."

"What?"

"You'll have to go to my hotel room and . . . get my gun."

"No!"

"Caroline."

"I will not! You are not going to face that man in the street tomorrow."

"What would you suggest I do, Caroline?"

"Tell the sheriff—"

"He did a lot of good last time, Caroline."

"I know, but . . ."

"But what? If I don't go out there, you heard what he said."

"So he'll burn us down. I'd rather lose this place than lose you."

"And what about Amanda?"

"I'll . . . send her to stay with a friend, or I'll—I'll" she stammered, but Clint cut her off.

"It won't stop with burning this place down, Caroline. They'll still come after me."

"Oh, Jesus!" she said, grabbing his arm and holding tightly to it. "What ever possessed you to take a steak knife . . . never mind. Never mind."

"Will you go and get my gun?"

She squeezed his arm even tighter and said in a barely audible tone, "Yes . . . yes, I'll get it, damn you!"

TWENTY-TWO

Caroline brought Clint his gun and his saddlebags, and he sat up in bed and cleaned the gun, making sure it was in working order. It had not been fired, and hardly touched, in six weeks.

Caroline sat and watched him work. What she hadn't told him was that she had stopped at the sheriff's office before going to his hotel . . .

"Hello, Miss Caroline," Leach said, failing to rise.

"Sheriff, I want you to know what happened at my café tonight."

"I know what happened."

"How?"

"I heard from someone who was there, and then I

109

talked to Doc. He patched up that fellow's hand, you know."

"No, I didn't know, and I don't care. Do you know what those men did?"

"Sure, they teased Adams a little, and he overreacted—"

"Overreacted?" she said in disbelief. "That man was going for his gun!"

"Look, Caroline, there's nothing I can do. If anything, the fella whose hand was injured could have pressed charges against Adams, but—"

"That's crazy. Look, he wants Clint to meet him in the street tomorrow. You've got to stop him."

He spread his hands helplessly and said again, "There's nothing I can do."

"Oh, like last time, huh?"

"Look," Leach said angrily, "I told Adams to leave town. I told him staying here would bring trouble. Now he's going to find out I was right."

She glared at him and said, "Well, I hope when someone gets killed tomorrow that you'll be satisfied with that," and she stalked out.

When Clint was done she said, "Can I get you anything? A cup of coffee?"

"No, nothing. Thanks." He holstered the gun and started to get up.

"Where are you going?"

"Back to my hotel."

"Oh, no, you're not," she said, putting her hands on his shoulders.

"I'm fine, Caroline—"

"You're safer here than you would be in your hotel."

"What makes you say that?"

"Those men might go into your hotel to try and get you tonight, but they wouldn't rush in here. Not with a woman and child present."

"Do you know what you're doing?"

"Yes."

"You're putting yourself and Amanda in jeopardy."

"No, I'm not. If you stay here, they won't be tempted to try and finish this tonight without waiting for tomorrow."

Clint studied her for a moment, then said, "You may be right. How did you get so smart?"

"If I was so smart I wouldn't have brought you your gun," she said.

He started to get up again and she said, "Now what?"

"I'm going to go and sleep on your couch—"

"No you're not," she said, pushing him back down again. "Will you please stop giving me a hard time. I'll sleep on the couch—much as I'd rather stay here with you."

Whenever they had sex it was in his hotel room, usually in the afternoon. They had never done it in her home, not with Amanda in another room.

"Now get some rest. I'll fix you breakfast in the morning."

He almost said something witty about killing or being killed on a full stomach, but decided that she wouldn't see the humor.

TWENTY-THREE

Breakfast was a very quiet affair. Even Amanda got up early to eat with Clint. No one spoke until they were finished eating, and then it was Caroline who broke the silence.

"Maybe they changed their minds," she said. "Maybe they left town."

"Sure," Clint said.

"Maybe the sheriff decided to . . ." she said, and then let it trail off.

"The sheriff? Did he get involved last night?"

"I, uh, understand that the doctor treated the man you injured, and spoke to the sheriff."

"You spoke to the sheriff, too, didn't you?" he asked. "When you went to get my gun."

She lowered her head and said, "Yes, I did."

"And what did he have to say?"

"He said that man could have pressed charges against you."

"Oh, I'm sure he said more than that, like how he warned me there'd be trouble?"

She nodded.

"And now I'd find out for myself? Right?"

Again, she nodded.

"Sure, he's going to take a lot of satisfaction in this."

"Especially if you get killed," Caroline said, then threw a quick look at Amanda. "Amanda . . ." she started to say, then decided to let the girl stay.

"I'm not going to get killed, Caroline," he said. "I haven't forgotten how to use a gun in six weeks."

"You can beat that man?"

"I'm sure I can," he said. What he didn't tell her was that he was also sure that he wouldn't be facing one man when he went out there, but all three.

While Caroline and Amanda took care of the dishes, Clint went out into the dining room and walked to the front window. Careful to stay out of sight, he took a look at the street and the rooftops across the way. He caught a glimpse of a man's hat up there and wondered what had caused him to go to the window at that particular time.

If there was one man on the roof across the street Clint was sure the other man would be on this side of the street. The big-mouth one called Kenny would be standing out in the street, probably using his mouth more than his gun to keep Clint occupied.

"What's wrong?" Caroline asked, coming up from behind him.

"Nothing," he said, turning to face her.

"You were looking at the roof across the street. Why?"

"Caroline—"

"One of the other men is up there, isn't he?" she asked, trying to get to the window. He took her by the shoulders to stop her.

"Don't get in front of the window."

"But if one of them is up there, how do you know both of them won't be? How do you know you won't be facing three—wait," she said, narrowing her eyes at him. "Wait, you knew, didn't you? You knew all along you'd be facing three men out there, didn't you?"

"Caroline—"

"Don't keep saying my name," she said, pulling away from him. "It's crazy for you to go out there and face three men."

"I've faced worse odds."

"Oh, sure, the Gunsmith has killed hundreds of men, hasn't he?" she said snappishly. "What's three more, right?"

"Car—" he started, and stopped short. "Look, I know they're up there," he said. "That gives *me* the edge. Don't you see?"

"No, I don't see," she said. "How the hell can you have an edge against three men?"

"My heart is pure."

She glared at him and said, "Damn you, Clint Adams," and then started to fight a smile that was tugging at the corners of her mouth. "If you go out there and get killed, I'll never forgive you."

"I accept that responsibility."

She moved into his arms then, nestling her head beneath his chin, and then they both heard the voice.

"Clint Adams!" the man named Kenny called out.

Clint and Caroline exchanged a glance then, remembering what happened the last time a man called to him like that.

"I'll get your gun," Caroline said, going into the kitchen.

Clint looked out the window and saw Kenny standing in the street. He had no qualms about facing Kenny. After all, he wasn't a Johnny Robak. Thinking back to Robak Clint tried to remember the man's move. What would have happened if Amanda hadn't run into the street, he wondered? Would the result have been different?

He decided not to dwell on that right now, not when there were three men waiting outside to kill him.

"Here," Caroline said, handing him his gunbelt.

Clint strapped it on for the first time in six weeks.

It felt fine.

TWENTY-FOUR

Clint stepped outside and Kenny grinned. Looking around, Clint could see that there was not the crowd that had watched him face Johnny Robak. There were several reasons for that.

This fella Kenny was not a Johnny Robak.

Clint Adams wasn't *the* Gunsmith anymore.

And the people obviously knew that there were two men on the rooftops with guns, and they didn't want to be anywhere near a crossfire.

He had no doubt that there were people watching from windows, however.

"Come on out, Gunsmith," Kenny said. Unlike Robak, Kenny didn't move toward the center of the street. He wanted to keep Clint's back to at least one of his friends on the roof. That meant that one of them was

117

on the roof of Caroline's Café. Talk about irony . . .

Clint stepped into the street and started moving to his right. By doing this he was forcing Kenny to turn to his left to face him. By the time Clint finished moving he was standing in the center of the street, confident that one gunman was to his right, and the other to his left.

"See this?" Kenny was saying. In fact, he had been talking the entire time, only Clint hadn't been listening. Now he was holding his bandaged left hand. "You're gonna pay for this . . ."

Clint decided not to wait for Kenny and his friends to make the first move.

He drew his gun, taking Kenny completely by surprise. He turned to his right and saw the man called Dale standing up on the roof. He fired once and, confident that his shot would be true, turned to his left just as Phil was taking a bead on him with a rifle. He fired once at Phil, and turned back in time to see Dale tumble from the top of his building. When he looked toward the roof of the café he didn't see anyone. Phil had either fled, or was lying on the roof, dead.

He looked at Kenny then, who had both hands out in front of him.

"Wait," he was saying breathlessly, "wait, wait . . ."

Clint walked toward the man with his gun in his hand, but held at his side.

"No, you can't," Kenny kept saying, "wait . . . please . . . listen . . ."

Clint stopped about ten feet away from Kenny and holstered his gun.

"It's your move, friend," he said.

"No, wait," Kenny said, waggling his hands in front of him now, "don't . . . don't . . ."

He started to backpedal then, moving away from

Clint with his hands still held in front of him, and then abruptly turned and started running up the street, shouting, "No, no, don't, don't . . ."

Slowly, doors opened and people stepped out of their homes and stores, and Sheriff Leach came out of his office. He said something to his deputy, who ran around behind the café, then started walking toward Clint.

The door to the café opened and both Caroline and Amanda came out slowly.

Clint walked over to the fallen Dale and rolled him over. The man was clearly dead, if not from the fall, than from the bullet in the center of his chest.

Sheriff Leach was walking down the street toward Clint when his deputy called from the roof of the café, "This one's dead, for sure."

Leach nodded and kept walking toward Clint. Clint decided not to wait for the man to speak.

"Don't say it, Leach," he said. "You could have stopped this."

"*You* could have *prevented* it from ever happening—" Leach began, but Clint just walked away from the man.

"Don't walk away from me!" Leach shouted, but Clint totally ignored him.

"Clint—" Caroline said.

"Come on," Clint said, "we've got a café to open."

The café did a booming business for lunch, and some people even asked Clint if he would wear his gun while he was serving them breakfast. He politely declined, and when the breakfast rush was over, he sat down to have a cup of coffee with Caroline.

"What does this mean, now?" Caroline asked.

"What should it mean?"

"Will you change your plans?"

"About staying?"

She nodded.

"No."

"What you did out there was . . . was amazing, and I respect you tremendously for not killing the third man."

"I didn't want to kill anyone."

"I realize that," she said, "but word will get around now, Clint. People will learn that you are not finished as the Gunsmith, unless . . ."

"Unless what?"

"Unless you hang up your gun."

"Hang it up? You mean, literally? A nail in the wall over there?" he asked, pointing.

"I didn't mean literally, but now that you mention it, maybe you should . . ."

"I don't think so."

"Why not?"

"Well, for one thing, it would be great for business, because people would want to come in and see the gun, right?"

"That's a reason not to do it?"

"Is that how you want to increase business?"

"Well, how different is that from what we have now? People coming in to be waited on by the Gunsmith. It's like a sideshow in here."

"I know . . ." he said. "I've been thinking about that." And he had been thinking about that, especially after what had happened today. Maybe it would be better if he did leave Newcombe's Flats—but did he want to leave Caroline and Amanda?

"Clint," she said, reaching across the table to cover one of his hands with one of hers, "you don't have to ask us. If you want to leave town, you can leave. If you want us to come with you, we'll come with you."

"You'd leave here? Leave your home?"

"It wouldn't be home once you left," Caroline said, "and I'm not saying anything about marriage. I'll put the café up for sale—"

"Let me think about it," Clint said. "We have plenty of time."

He took her hand for a moment, and then released it.

"I have to get ready for lunch," she said.

"I'll finish the pot and bring it in."

She nodded and went into the kitchen.

Clint poured himself another cup of coffee and looked around him. After being out in the street the walls of the café seemed to be a lot closer than they had been.

That scared him.

TWENTY-FIVE

Johnny Robak was in New Mexico when he read about Clint Adams in the papers. According to the report, the Gunsmith had faced three men and killed two of them, letting the other get away. Robak closed the paper, set it aside, and continued to eat his breakfast.

This was even better than he thought.

Not only was Adams still alive, but he was apparently healthy and still fairly proficient with a gun. Of course, he probably wasn't as good as he had once been, or he wouldn't have let the third man get away. Still, this time when Robak outdrew him and killed him, there would at least be no talk about the Gunsmith not being able to defend himself.

In Johnny Robak's mind, the little girl who had crossed the street between he and Clint Adams that day did not exist. He had convinced himself that he would have outdrawn Clint Adams, anyway. He had no fear whatsoever about facing the Gunsmith again.

In fact, he was looking forward to it. He wished he could face someone like the Gunsmith every few months or so. Just the thought of it invigorated him, brought him back to life.

After breakfast Robak was going to go and find himself a woman. He was sure that the local whore-house would open early for the man who had shot the Gunsmith.

TWENTY-SIX

A week went by since the shooting in the street and Clint and Caroline never again discussed leaving New-combe's Flats. They were both still thinking about it, though.

Caroline wanted to leave because she could see how unhappy Clint was becoming. He was not the kind of man who would be satisfied waiting tables. The novelty had long since worn off for him. She loved him so much that she would have been in favor of his leaving on his own, if it made him happy.

She was afraid, however, to ask him if that was what he wanted to do.

Amanda loved Clint and wanted him to be her father. She wondered why he and her mother hadn't gotten married yet. If it was obvious to her—a little girl—that

125

they loved each other, then why wasn't it obvious to them?

Grown-ups were so confusing.

Clint Adams was beginning to feel hemmed in.

He was in his hotel room, waiting for Caroline to come. Amanda was in school, and this was the only time they had to share a bed together. They usually closed the café for an hour or so, sometimes longer. Business had gotten so good that they could actually afford to do so.

Clint was staring out the window at the street, where he'd stood a week ago and faced three men.

For years he had wanted to be rid of his reputation. He felt that it was like a weight on his shoulders that he had to carry around with him all the time, getting heavier every year.

Then suddenly, through an accident, his reputation had been taken from him. Suddenly, the weight was gone, and he was glad. He had survived the incident, he had found Caroline and Amanda, both of whom he cared for very much. He had actually thought he'd be satisfied with becoming Caroline's partner in the café, working there, and staying in Newcombe's Flats.

Since the incident on the street, though, suddenly the town seemed small, the café seemed ever smaller. He resented having to wait on people who were there only so they could say they were served by a man who was once famous. That was before the shooting. Now since the shooting they were coming in the hopes that he'd wear his gun while he served them.

Even after killing two men and driving the third away, he was not getting any respect from the people in town. He still did not have his reputation, and he'd never realized before that if the rep went, so would respect.

The rep had never been important to him, but he had always felt that respect was.

Now he had neither, but in order to get one back, did he have to get the other, as well?

He had received several telegraph messages from friends, most notably from Rick Hartman, who was asking when he was coming to Labyrinth. He hadn't been able to answer that, but suddenly he felt that a trip to Labyrinth was in order.

The last time his life had been in such a mess had been immediately following Bill Hickok's death. Labyrinth had been the place where he'd pulled himself back together.

Maybe he needed to go there again . . . but maybe there was something else he had to do first.

How could he explain all of this to Caroline? How could he make her understand that he needed some time away from Newcombe's Flats, from her and Amanda, time to think about what was best for him?

How could he tell her that he needed to leave town and try to find Johnny Robak so he could finish what they had started months ago?

After they made love he tried to explain everything to her, and to her credit she remained silent and let him get it all out.

"When will you leave?" she asked.

Just like that. No recriminations, no tears, just a simple question.

"I don't know," he said. "The end of the week, I guess. I'll have to send a few telegraph messages to try and locate Robak."

"And when you meet, either you'll kill him or he'll kill you."

"That would seem to be the only way it could possibly go."

"What if he doesn't want to face you, this time? I mean, he's beaten you once, why should he try again?"

"Because he didn't kill me, and because he's probably read about what happened here by now. He'll feel that he can't really feel like a legend unless he kills me."

"Why not just wait here for him to get here?"

Clint thought that one over and said, "I'd rather this confrontation didn't take place here."

"Why?"

He shrugged.

"Superstitious."

He didn't know if that was true or not. He'd never been superstitious before, he only knew that he didn't want to have to think about last time, and that'd be hard not to do if they were standing on the same street.

"Will you come back once you've made up your mind?" she asked.

"Of course," he said. "Whatever I've decided, I'll come back and talk to you about it."

"All right, then," she said. "The first thing I'll have to do is hire a waiter, although when people see you're not there they'll probably stop coming."

"Oh, I don't know. You underestimate the power of your cooking."

"All I know," she said, swinging her legs to the floor, "is that it can't keep you here."

He didn't have anything to say to that, so he stood up and they dressed in silence. Clint knew that he had probably changed things between them, no matter what he decided, but he didn't feel like he had a legitimate choice in the matter. He had to go and, hopefully, he would come back.

TWENTY-SEVEN

When they left his hotel Clint told Caroline that he would meet her at the café. They separated and he went to the telegraph office.

The first message he sent was to Rick Hartman. Hartman, though based in Labyrinth, Texas, seemed to have an inexhaustible supply of informants around the country, and Clint felt sure that he would be able to pinpoint Johnny Robak's location to some degree.

After that he sent a message to Bat Masterson, and Wyatt Earp, and some of his other friends who had sent him their good wishes. He felt badly that he had not done so much earlier.

That done, he decided to go over to the livery to look in on Duke.

" 'Afternoon, Mr. Adams," the liveryman said. "Checking on him?"

"Just came by to see if the big boy was doing all right, Virgil."

"I been treating him right, you know that," the older man said eagerly.

"I know it , Virgil. I'm getting ready to take a long trip at the end of the week. I just wanted to let him know."

"He does understand you when you talk to him, don't he?" Virgil asked. "Sometimes I feel like he's watching me, and he knows what I'm doing. He sure does seem to be a smart horse."

"That he is, Virgil."

Clint went to the back stall and stepped in with Duke.

"Whaddaya say, big boy?"

Duke shook his massive head in greeting.

"We're going to be taking a long ride at the end of the week, fella, so you'll be getting lots of exercise. I know you miss traveling."

What about himself, he wondered. Was that part of his unease of late? Did he miss the traveling, as well? Yeah, he probably did.

"It's hard to shake, isn't it, big fella?" he said, patting the gelding's huge neck. "That wanderlust gets into your blood."

Duke nodded his agreement.

"Yeah, you want to get going, don't you? Maybe I've been wrong hanging around here so long, putting myself out on display like a freak."

Again Duke nodded in agreement—or moved his head to dislodge a fly.

"All right," Clint said, slapping Duke's rump. "I've given you something to look forward to, so be a good fella and show some patience."

But as he walked out of the livery he realized that Duke wasn't the impatient one, he was.

He stopped off at the telegraph office on the way to the café and found a reply from Rick Hartman. Rick promised to burn up the wires and have a general location on Johnny Robak by the following day—or so.

As long as Clint had some idea of what direction to go in when he left Newcombe's Flats, he'd be satisfied.

When he entered the café he heard pots being banged around in the kitchen and went to see what the racket was all about. He pushed aside the curtain and watched while Caroline seemed to move pots around haphazardly, slamming them down and against each other.

"What's going on?"

She turned swiftly, her eyes wet with tears. Frantically she wiped her eyes with her hands.

"You startled me."

"You're crying."

"A woman has a right to cry," she said, "even if it's for no reason."

"You don't cry for no reason."

She stared at him, then turned her back and said, "No, you're right, I don't cry for no reason."

"Then . . . why?" he asked, feeling foolish for asking. Obviously he had made her cry.

She turned to face him when she felt she had herself under control.

"You've never asked me about my husband."

That took him aback.

"Uh, no, I haven't."

"Why not?"

"I didn't feel it was important," he said.

"What do you think happened to him?"

"I assumed that . . . you were a widow."

"Well, you assumed wrong," she said. "My husband left us when Amanda was two. He said he wasn't ready to be a father. As far as I'm concerned, he was never ready to be a husband, either. I cried then, too, when he left, but soon realized I was crying for nothing."

"And now you think I'm leaving."

"But that's stupid, don't you see? We're not married, we haven't even made any commitment other than as business partners, so what the hell am I crying about?"

"Caroline . . ." he said, feeling somewhat helpless, "I can't . . ."

She held up her hand to stop him.

"I'm not asking for a commitment. I don't have any right."

"Of course you do," he said. "You're the main reason I'm up and around now."

"I did that because I wanted to," she said. "I wanted to help you. Oh, in the beginning I felt guilty because it was Amanda . . . but later, I did it because I wanted to. When someone does something because they want to, then the other person doesn't owe them anything. I didn't do it because I was hoping you'd fall in love with me and decide to stay here with me and Amanda. I . . . I'm rambling on like some crazy woman, aren't I?"

"No, you're not . . ."

She waved away his denial and said, "I've got to get lunch started. Clint, you do what you think you have to do. You have that right."

He heard someone enter the café and said, "Well, right now I've got to be a waiter."

"Fine, a customer. That's what we need, customers.

Let's get this lunchtime underway."

Clint nodded, but Caroline had already turned her back and was moving pots on the stove, this time with more purpose and less noise.

He went to take the customer's order . . .

TWENTY-EIGHT

After the dinner crowd faded to one lone diner, Clint went into the kitchen, looking for Amanda.

"Where's Amanda?"

"Upstairs."

"This early?"

Caroline looked at Clint.

"I told her you were leaving."

Clint made a face.

"I wish you had left that to me, Caroline."

"She's my daughter," she snapped, and then she relented and said, "She knew something was wrong, Clint."

"She's a smart girl."

"That she is."

"Should I go up and talk to her?"

"No," Caroline said. "I explained the situation, and told her that you would be back. Give her some time to herself. Talk to her tomorrow."

"All right."

They both heard the door open and close, and Clint looked out to see if the last diner had left without paying. He had not. The man was still enjoying his stew, and there was another man in the room.

Sheriff Pete Leach.

"Good evening, Sheriff," Clint said. "Taking dinner here, tonight?"

"I had an urge for some of Caroline's stew," Leach said, taking a table. "I'm not too late, am I?"

"No, of course not. I'll bring it out."

He went into the kitchen and told Caroline that Leach was there for dinner.

"He's got some nerve."

"He appreciates your cooking," he said. "Give the man a break."

"How can you say that after all he's done—or not done."

"I said you should give him a break," Clint said, accepting the bowl of stew, "that doesn't mean I'm going to."

He brought the sheriff his stew, and then made one more trip to bring him some bread and a beer.

"Have a seat, Adams," the sheriff said.

"I'm not supposed to sit with the customers."

"I know the boss, so don't worry about it."

Clint sat across from the man.

"I understand you're leaving at the end of the week."

"Virgil on your payroll?"

Leach laughed.

"Virgil doesn't have to be on anyone's payroll to talk.

He just naturally tells whatever he knows."

Clint knew that was true.

"Where you heading?"

"Why is that your concern?"

"I'm not concerned," Leach said. "I'm curious."

"Eat it," Clint said.

"The stew?"

"Your curiosity," Clint said, standing up.

"You're going to look for Robak, aren't you?"

Clint didn't reply.

"I figured you'd get tired of waiting tables and playing house—"

Clint reached down and grabbed ahold of Leach's shirt. He had lost some weight due to his injury, but he almost effortlessly hauled Leach to his feet.

"Hey, my dinner—" Leach said.

"You're finished," Clint said. He turned the sheriff around, grabbed him by the neck and the back of the belt, and propelled him toward the door.

"You can't do this," Leach said. "I'm the law."

"That can change, too, Leach," Clint said. "What would you say if I decided to stay and run against you in the next election?"

Leach pulled free at the door and turned around.

"You wouldn't!"

"Keep pushing me, then. Just be satisfied that I'm riding out at the end of the week, but remember this."

"What?"

Clint grinned and said, "I'm coming back real soon."

Leach frowned, then said, "I could haul you in for what you did."

Clint smiled now and pointed to a sign over the door. It said: WE RESERVE THE RIGHT TO REFUSE SERVICE AT OUR DISCRETION.

"Badge or no badge," Clint added.

Leach read the sign again, then hitched up his belt and left.

"What happened?" Caroline asked.

The last diner said, "Clint tossed the sheriff out."

"And I missed it?" Caroline said.

"It was something to see," the other man said, grinning. His name was Albert, and he ate dinner in the café about three times a week, or whenever he had enough money for a meal.

"Hey, Clint?"

"Yes, Albert?"

Albert pointed to the sheriff's untouched stew.

"You gonna throw that out?"

Clint picked up the bowl of stew, put it in front of Albert, and said, "Be my guest, Albert."

"Clint?"

Clint turned away from the front door, which he was locking, and looked at Caroline.

"Yes?"

"I think we should look for a waiter to replace you tomorrow, and then you can start concerning yourself with . . . what you have to do."

"I can work until the end of the week—"

"We can use the time to show the new person the ropes."

"Does it have to be a waiter?" he asked.

"No, we can hire a waitress just as well. Why, you have someone in mind?"

"No," he said, "I just wanted to be clear on it."

"Now that you mention it," she said, "I might have someone in mind. You know Mrs. Malcolm, who runs the dress shop?"

"Sure."

"She has a sixteen-year-old daughter, Hannah. I think I could get her."

"Well, that's fine."

"So you can start planning for your trip."

"Nothing to plan," he said. "I'll take Duke and leave my rig here. I'll go to the general store the day before I leave and pick up some dry goods."

"I can pack you some chicken for the first day."

"That'd be great," he said. She was talking like he was going away on a cattle-buying trip and she was packing for him.

"Is your gun, uh, okay?"

"My gun is fine," he said.

"And your rifle?"

"I'll clean both of my guns before I leave. They'll both be fine."

"Good."

There was an awkward silence then, which Caroline finally broke somewhat lamely.

"You see, I'm really dealing with this."

"I can see that."

"Your last night here?"

"Yes?"

"I can get someone to stay with Amanda."

He went to her and put his hand to her cheek.

"Going to make it hard for me to leave, huh?"

She took his hand in hers and said, "As goddam hard as I possibly can."

TWENTY-NINE

Johnny Robak was in a whorehouse in Claxton, New Mexico, enjoying the attention of a chubby brunette. This was just a stopover on his trip back to Newcombe's Flats, which would probably take him another nine days or so. With each passing day he was looking more and more forward to arriving. He hoped to be able to take care of the Gunsmith immediately, and get out again. He didn't think that sheriff would want him to stay around once he killed Clint Adams.

The brunette was crouched between his legs, her mouth full, gobbling his penis greedily and noisily. He had requested that she do it with as much noise as possible, and she was certainly doing her job. In fact, if he didn't know better he would have thought that his penis was the best thing she'd tasted in months.

He cupped his hands on her head as she continued to suck him, and he eased her off him and told her to lie down.

She had big breasts, which fell to either side of her as she laid back, and he slid between her legs and rammed his penis home.

He proceeded to plow, resting comfortably on her opulent curves, driving his rock-hard penis into her over and over again, as she reclined beneath him, moaning and groaning appreciatively and expertly.

"Gee, honey," she said moments later, "that was just great. You're really—"

He cut her off by backhanding her across the face.

"I'm paying for the use of your body, bitch, not to listen to your whore talk," he said. "Save it for somebody who needs it."

"You can't hit me—"

"I just did," he said, reminding her, "and I'll do it again if you don't shut up."

She thought about objecting further, but decided it would be healthier not to.

Robak stood up to get dressed, and the girl watched in silence. She was rubbing her cheek, hoping that she wouldn't bruise.

"Here," Robak said, throwing the girl some money.

"You're supposed to pay downstairs."

"I will," Robak said. "That's for you."

"Gee, thanks, mister—"

"Just shut up," he said. "That's what the money is for."

She opened her mouth to speak, then abruptly closed it and simply nodded her head.

As he left the whorehouse after settling with the madam—"Yeah, yeah, she was great"—he heard a voice from behind him as he started to cross the street.

"Robak! Johnny Robak!"

Robak turned and almost expected to see Clint Adams standing there. It wasn't Adams, though, it was some wet-behind-the-ears kid sporting what looked like a brand-new gun. Upon closer inspection, it turned out to be a silver-plated gun with pearl handles.

Jesus, Robak thought. It occurred to him that he hadn't had anything to eat, and his stomach was feeling queasy from the three beers.

"Are you Robak?"

"That's me," Robak said.

"The man who outdrew the Gunsmith?"

"That's right." Come on, come on, kid, get to it already.

A crowd started to gather on both sides of the street. Robak wondered how long it would take for a badge to make an appearance.

"Well, mister, I owe you for that."

Robak sighed.

"Was Adams a friend of yours, son?"

"No, he wasn't a friend. I'm the man who was gonna outdraw him."

"Never in a million years, sonny."

"Oh, yeah? Well, now that you outdrew him, I'll just have to outdraw you."

"That's even less likely."

"You just get ready," the kid said, going into his most convincing gunfighter pose. He spread his legs, dangled his arm at his side, and narrowed his eyes.

"Kid, I'm always ready," Robak said, and he drew and shot the kid through the chest before the boy had a chance to touch that fancy gun.

Jesus, Robak thought, turning away and holstering

his gun, did Adams have to put up with assholes like that all those years?

He should be glad he won't have to anymore. Robak was going to put Clint Adams someplace where he wouldn't ever have to worry about kids like that again.

And he wouldn't have to worry about sour stomachs from no food and stale beer, either.

THIRTY

While Caroline got Amanda off to school—after which she was going to talk to Hannah Malcolm about a job as a waitress—Clint went to the telegraph office to see if there was a reply from Rick Hartman yet. He didn't really expect to find one this early, so he was very pleasantly surprised when he found it waiting for him.

CLINT, ROBAK SEEN IN MEXICO, HEADING FOR NEW MEXICO. LOOKS TO BE HEADED IN YOUR DIRECTION. LUCK.

R.H.

Clint thought it over for a moment. If Robak was heading his way, all he had to do was to start from this end, and sooner or later they'd meet on a trail, or in a

145

town. He wouldn't even have to look for Robak. They'd just run into each other.

Anxious now to leave, Clint decided to go ahead and wait the extra two days as originally planned. He didn't want to disappoint Caroline and Amanda any more than he already had.

That reminded him, too, that he had to talk to Amanda, today, and make sure she understood—as well as a little girl her age could understand.

At the end of the school day Clint walked to the schoolhouse to meet Amanda. The little girl saw him and reacted with surprise, stopping for a moment, and then continued to walk toward him.

"What are you doing here?" she asked him, very seriously.

"I wanted to come and meet you."

"Why?"

"So we could talk."

"About what?"

"I think you know."

She looked down at the ground, and then looked up at him again.

"You mean about you leaving?"

"That's right."

"What do you want to talk about?"

"Well . . . I just want to make sure that you understand why I'm going. Let's walk."

They began to walk and Amanda said, "I understand why you're going."

"You do?"

"Yes," she said, nodding her head.

He waited to see if she was going to offer anything more, and then asked, "Well, why?"

"Because you want to kill that man who shot you."

He started to object, and then stopped. Put in its simplest form, that was exactly why he was leaving. How could he tell her it was not?

"Did your mother tell you that?"

"No. I figured it out myself. I'm not stupid, you know."

"Oh, I know that," he said.

"Will you be coming back?"

"Yes."

"If you're still alive, right? If that man doesn't shoot you again."

"That's right."

He had started to talk to her as if she was a little girl, and now she was talking to him as if she was an adult. Was it any wonder that he loved her?

She stopped walking and looked up at him. Suddenly, she was a little girl again.

"You can't promise that you'll come back, can you?"

"No, honey, I can't. I can only promise that if I am physically able, I'll come back."

"Well," she said after a moment, "I guess I can't ask for more than that, can I?"

"Nope, you sure can't."

She took his hand then and said, "Let's go home."

THIRTY-ONE

The last night he was to be in town Caroline had someone stay with Amanda so she could spend the night with Clint.

"How is Hannah working out?" Clint asked.

"She's doing fine."

The small talk out of the way, they went to bed.

"I'm not going to cry," she said after they'd made love the first time.

"Well, good," he said.

"I mean it. I swore I wouldn't cry tonight."

"I'm glad to hear it," Clint said. "Because if you start, I might start."

"That might be worth seeing."

"Stop it," he said, tightening his arm around her.

"Oh, Clint," she said, sighing, "I don't know how to thank you."

"For what?"

"For six weeks of someone to love."

"You have Amanda."

"Yes, and I love her dearly, but you know that's not the same thing."

"I know."

"I know that you love her."

He hesitated a moment, then said, "Yes, I do. I admitted that to myself today."

There was a long silence then. Clint knew that she was wondering if he loved her, and he was wondering the same thing, himself. Finally, neither of them brought it up.

"She's going to miss you."

"And I'll miss her. Can we not do this?"

"I'm sorry," she said, turning toward him. "I really didn't mean to be like this tonight."

"How did you mean to be?" he asked, hugging her.

Her hand slid down between their bodies and grabbed his semierect penis.

"Like this," she said, sliding down under the sheet.

He felt the heat of her mouth engulf him, and he closed his eyes . . .

In the morning she walked him to the livery stable and watched while he saddled Duke.

"Why can't he stand still?" she asked as Duke kept shifting and moving.

"He's in a hurry to be going," Clint said.

"Then he and you are a lot alike."

He turned to face her and said, "I guess so."

She moved to him and into the circle of his arms.

They stood like that for a few moments, and then she backed away.

"All right, go and do what you have to do. Amanda and I will be here when you get back."

Clint had said good-bye to Amanda the night before, and like her mother, she had not cried, either.

Clint walked Duke out of the livery, followed by Caroline. He mounted up and rode out without looking back.

She had told him to do that the night before. She said that if it was the last time she ever saw him, she did not want it to be looking back.

He didn't understand it, but he agreed.

The first night out, Clint camped by a stream and prepared a pot of coffee. He had only brought with him some beef jerky for the trip, but on this night he had some fried chicken that Caroline had wrapped up for him.

He sat and ate the chicken with the coffee. He didn't feel bad considering this had been his first full day in the saddle. The only soreness he felt was in his chest, but that was to be expected. Although the wound had been high up on the left side, the soreness, when it came, spread through the entire chest. He knew that when he woke up in the morning the soreness would be all but gone, but he wondered how his back would be after having slept in a bed for close to seven weeks.

He had thoroughly enjoyed the day's ride. He knew now how much he missed the traveling and that he'd never be able to settle down in Newcombe's Flats, with or without Caroline and Amanda Fleming. All he had to do now was convince them that it was no fault or failure on their part.

Did he love Caroline? With this distance between them, he was able to admit that he did not. He had strong feelings for her, feelings of affection, but he didn't love her—not in the way a woman like her deserved to be loved.

As for Amanda, he did love her, but that certainly wasn't enough to make him stay put. He'd miss her, but she needed a father, and with him gone, maybe Caroline would finally meet someone who would become Amanda's new father.

He felt free now. He knew that when he finished with Johnny Robak he'd go back to Newcombe's Flats to get his rig and team and would be on his way.

He'd probably go back to Labyrinth, Texas, for a rest in a place where he knew he'd never be pressured or challenged. If and when he did settle down, it would probably be in Labyrinth. Maybe he'd even take Rick Hartman up on his constant offer to become his business partner.

First, though, Johnny Robak.

THIRTY-TWO

Three days after leaving Newcombe's Flats Clint was in New Mexico. The first town he came to was called Ratona, which was spitting distance from the Texas Panhandle.

Ratona was a fair-sized town, and Clint was hoping for a decent meal and some good coffee. He'd been spoiled by Caroline's cooking, but if he found a steak that was hot and chewable, he would be satisfied.

He left Duke in the livery and went to Ratona's only hotel.

"Seems a fair-sized town to have one hotel," Clint said to the clerk as he was signing in.

"I wouldn't mind if I had the money to expand," the man said. He was a middle-aged man who was apparently the owner of the hotel. "Fact is, they're getting

153

ready to build another one at the other end of town. Staying long?"

"Overnight."

The man nodded and handed Clint a key.

"Where can I get a decent steak?"

"Down the street at Jerry's, or right here in the dining room."

"Which is better?"

"Please," the man said, "you're putting me in an awkward position."

Clint laughed and said, "Can I get a bath?"

"Sure, whenever you want."

"Well, how about in ten minutes?"

"It'll be ready."

"Fine," Clint said. "I'll just drop my gear off in the room."

"Yes, sir. Top of the stairs, turn right, and it's at the end of the hall. Your room overlooks the main street."

"Thanks," Clint said. He slung his saddlebags over his shoulder and picked up his Winchester.

In his room—which was nice, although it couldn't match the opulence of San Francisco, or even Sacramento hotels—he dropped the saddlebags on the bed and laid the rifle against the wall. He took off his gunbelt and hung it on the bedpost.

Clint walked to the window and saw that it did indeed overlook the main street.

He stretched, reaching up over his head, and held that position until the muscles in his back creaked, and then turned and walked to the bed, rubbing his chest absently. He removed his modified Colt from his holster, considered cleaning it now, and then decided to wait until after a bath and dinner. He slid the gun back into the leather, took the holster from the bedpost and carried it out of the room with him. When he bathed, it would rest handy on a chair right next to the bathtub.

Old habits died hard.

He went downstairs and the clerk said, "Your bath is waiting, Mr. . . . Adams?" He had to look at the register to recall Clint's name, but suddenly he seemed to recognize it, and threw Clint a wary look. "Would there be anything else I could do for you, uh, sir?"

"No, thanks," Clint said, "I think I'll just have that bath."

"Of course. Right through that curtain, first door on the left."

Clint went through the curtain, looked to his left and as he pushed the door open he noticed that there was no lock on it. Inside he saw a metal bathtub filled three quarters, and one straight-backed wooden chair. He had a decision to make. Should he put the chair against the door with the back of it jammed beneath the doorknob, or should he put it next to the tub so that his gun would be easily within reach? He finally opted for the gun. He didn't think anyone else would be coming in for a bath at this time of the evening.

He undressed, positioned the chair to his liking, laid his gunbelt on top of his clothing, and then eased himself into the tub.

The water was tepid at best, but he decided not to complain. He settled in, not relaxing completely—he never relaxed completely—but enough to ease some of the travel weariness in his muscles. The doctor had told him that hot baths would help the soreness in his chest. He didn't know how helpful this particular bath would be in that respect, but at least he'd get clean. This was his first stop in a town since he'd left Newcombe's Flats.

Hot water would have kept him in the tub longer, and

he did want to eat, so he quickly soaped the trail dust off of himself and then stood, reaching for the towel that wasn't there. He'd forgotten to ask for one, and the clerk had obviously forgotten to supply one.

He stepped out of the tub, started for the door, stepped outside and then stopped when he heard the commotion.

Something was going on in the lobby of the hotel. He could hear the loud voices of at least two men, and then a woman cried out, as if in pain. Clint went back into the room, snatched up his gun and ran back into the hallway, unmindful of his nakedness.

After all, a woman had screamed—or at least, cried out—and old habits died hard.

He hurried down the hall toward the lobby and when he came through the curtained doorway he saw a dark-haired young woman being cornered by three men. The clerk was on the floor in front of the desk. He'd obviously been knocked down when he tried to help the woman.

Three men, all dressed in trail clothes, were either ranch hands or they were passing through. In either case, they were forcing their attentions on a woman who obviously wanted no part of them.

One of them had her by the arms and she was trying without success to disengage herself. Another had his hands on her body, obviously enjoying the way she felt. The third man—much larger than the first two—was behind the first two, trying to get his hands in as well.

"Hold it!" Clint called out.

The three men looked his way and were obviously amused by what they saw.

"Better go back to your bath, mister," one of them said.

The woman looked at him, pleading with her eyes.

"Let her go."

"This ain't none of your affair, mister. Don't try dealing yourself in."

"I'm not dealing myself in," Clint said, raising his gun from behind the desk so they could see it, "I'm dealing you boys out."

The spokesman—the man who was holding the woman's arm's—turned his head and looked at the third man, nodding. He was obviously the one the other two looked to for their instructions.

The third man turned toward Clint and started to advance on him. He was a big man, huge across the chest and shoulders, and made no move to go for his gun.

"Moose is gonna break your back, mister. You can kill him if you want, but his gun is holstered, and we got witnesses that'll say you gunned him."

"I won't kill him," Clint said.

The first man smiled and Moose flexed his huge hands in anticipation.

"But I will stop him," Clint said.

With that he fired, shooting the big man in the left leg, just above the knee. He could have shot him *in* the knee, but he really had no desire to cripple the man.

Moose staggered as the bullet hit him, frowned, and then went down, sitting on the floor next to the clerk. He grabbed his leg and began to moan.

"What the—" the first man said.

"Let the woman go."

"Mister, you just bought yourself a pack of trouble," the man said, but he did let the woman go, as did the second man. She hurriedly put some distance between herself and them as they turned to face Clint.

"I won't be as generous with you boys as I was with your friend," Clint said. He cocked the hammer back on his gun and said, "I'll kill both of you."

Apprehension appeared in the eyes of both men.

"Pick up your friend and get out," Clint said.

They hesitated only a second before helping Moose to his feet, staggering under his weight. The clerk also got to his feet and moved toward the desk.

"You ain't heard the last of this, Mister," the first man blustered.

"Just keep walking, son," Clint called out. He eased the hammer back down on his gun as they went through the door.

He turned to find both the clerk and the woman staring at him. The woman was trying to keep her eyes averted, and in spite of the very recent incident, was also trying to keep from laughing aloud.

It was then that Clint remembered he was naked.

"Are you all right?" he asked the clerk.

"Uh, I'm fine, sir. I was trying—"

"Then get me a towel, damn it!" Clint said. "And make it quick!"

The man perked up and said, "Right away, sir."

Clint turned and hurried through the curtained doorway just as the woman lost control and began laughing aloud.

THIRTY-THREE

Clint was having dinner in the hotel dining room when he saw the woman come into the room. He hadn't had a real good look at her in the hotel lobby, but he knew it was the same woman. He hoped she wouldn't come his way.

She looked around the room, and when the waiter came to her and offered her one of the many empty tables that were available, she shook her head and pointed to Clint. The waiter nodded and walked to Clint's table.

"Excuse me, sir, but the lady at the door wants me to ask you if you would mind if she joined you?"

Clint looked at her now and saw that she was young and pretty.

"Would you?" he asked the waiter.

The waiter looked at the girl, then back at Clint and said, "No, sir."

"Well then . . ." Clint said. When the man continued to look at him uncomprehendingly, Clint said, "Tell the lady I'd be honored."

"Yes, sir."

The waiter relayed his message, and then showed the woman to Clint's table.

"Excuse me . . ." she said.

Clint pushed his chair back and stood up. Up close he could see that she was in her early twenties, *very* pretty, with chestnut-colored hair and a slim figure. He was surprised at how embarrassed he felt that this woman had seen him naked earlier.

"My name is Adams, miss, Clint Adams."

"I'm Sherry Logan, Mr. Adams. I owe you my thanks, and my apology. May I sit and join you?"

"Please."

As she sat the waiter said, "Dinner, ma'am?"

She hesitated a moment, then said, "Bring me what the gentleman is having."

"Yes, ma'am."

When the waiter left Clint was at a loss for words, so he waited for her to speak.

"I never thanked you for helping me earlier today. You were very . . . brave."

"Not really," he said. "I had the drop on them."

"But there were three of them. It takes a brave man to face three men on behalf of someone he doesn't know."

"If you say so."

"Also, I should apologize for laughing at you."

"Why should you?" he asked. "I must have looked pretty funny."

She smiled and said, "Yes, you did."

"Well, when you see something funny, you laugh."

"I must tell you," she said, "I was so frightened by those men, but when I saw you standing there . . . naked . . . I just had to laugh, and all my fear just left me."

"Well, I'm glad."

"So I should thank you twice."

"Maybe you should just stop thanking me and we'll talk about something else."

Her dinner came while they were exchanging small talk, and they just continued on in that vein. Clint was wondering what she really wanted, and was only half-listening to her.

After dinner they shared a pot of coffee, and when it was time to leave she insisted on paying.

"Really," she said, "I feel that I must."

"All right," he said, relenting. "Thank you."

She paid and they went out into the lobby together.

"Are you going up to your room?" she asked.

"Yes."

Without hesitating she said, "May I accompany you?"

For a moment he wasn't sure he'd heard her right. Then he figured he'd heard her right, but maybe he was misinterpreting her words.

"I'm sorry . . ."

"I want to come to your room with you, Clint. I want to truly show you my gratitude."

"Sherry, you don't have to—"

"I'm also alone in this town, and what happened earlier has thrown a scare into me. I don't really want to be alone tonight."

"Well," he said, "I guess I could sleep on the floor—"

"Please," she said, "you're misunderstanding me. I

want to share a bed with you. I want to be with you. I want to make love with you."

Now there was no possibility of error.

"I don't know what to say," he said.

"Is there any reason why you wouldn't want to make love with me?" she asked. "Am I not attractive enough?"

"You're extremely attractive, and very desirable," Clint said.

"Well then . . . ?"

Clint thought it over very quickly. There was no reason in the world why he shouldn't take this girl into his room. He'd spent the past seven weeks with Caroline, although they had only been lovers for less than half that time. Still, the fact that they were lovers did not prevent him from sleeping with another woman. He'd slept with many women in his life, for one reason or another, but usually because they appealed to him.

This woman appealed to him.

"All right," he said, "let's go upstairs."

THIRTY-FOUR

Her breasts were small but firm, with unusually large
nipples and aurcola for their size. The dark circles of her
nipples seemed to cover almost half her breasts.

"I know," she said, "they're funny-looking."

"No, they're not," he said.

They had undressed and slid into bed together, and
for the first few moments they inspected each other's
bodies. He had been studying her breasts, while her eyes
had been drawn to the scar on his chest.

"They're beautiful," he told her, and bent to kiss them
each in turn. She shuddered gently, then ran her hand
over the scar, where the flesh of the wound was still
pink.

"This is recent."

"Yes."

"It must have been terribly serious."

"It's high on the left side," he said. "If it had been lower, it would have been more serious."

She leaned over and ran her mouth over it gently, then used her tongue. She reached between his legs then and took hold of his penis, which was swelling as she held it. She bent over and slid her mouth over the head and felt it grow in her mouth. She licked it wetly, stroking it gently with her hand.

He looked down at her head in his lap and wondered if he should be feeling any guilt. He had only left Caroline's bed three days ago, and he knew she was waiting for him to come back.

Sherry's mouth suddenly encompassed most of his length and he caught his breath. She moaned appreciatively as she sucked him, and her expertise belied the innocence of her pretty face. She cupped his testicles, fondling them gently, and began using her mouth and both hands to bring him right to the brink of climax.

He pulled her off of him then and began to inspect her body with his mouth and tongue. He worked his way down between her legs, where her pubic hair was lighter than the hair on her head, almost red. He ran his tongue along her moist slit and heard her catching her breath, then probed her gently, tasting her while she writhed a bit on the bed, moving her butt back and forth. Finally his tongue contacted her clit and she jumped, letting out a high-pitched moan. He circled her clit with his tongue, slowly at first, then increasingly faster, and she finally grabbed his head and wrapped his hair around her fingers as she rode the wave of her climax.

"Oh, Lordy, that was sweet," she said as he laid down next to her.

"So are you," he said, licking her right breast.

She was extremely sweet, and he continued to lick both of her breasts, enjoying the salt of her perspiration. She moaned and groped for him, drawing him over her, and then opened her legs so he could enter her.

"Ooh, yes, yes," she said, digging her heels into his buttocks.

He began to take her in long, easy strokes as she whispered in his ear, and then he slid his hands beneath her to cup her small buttocks and pull her to him as he pushed into her. He did her this way for a few minutes, never varying the tempo, and then felt her begin to tremble. Now he increased his rhythm, driving into her, bringing her to him, and when he felt her climax he held her tightly to him and exploded into her . . .

He woke once during the night with her head between his legs again. When she saw that he was awake she climbed atop him, lifted her hips and then eased down onto the length of him, taking him into her steaming womanhood slowly, inch by inch.

"Oh, yes," she said when she sat down flat on him, her buttocks resting on his upper thighs.

He pulled her down so he could suck on her nipples as she rode him, and when the sensations became too much for her to bear she sat up straight, throwing her head back and bouncing on him madly. Her second orgasm did not come as easily as the first, and he had to work hard to stay with her, so that when she finally did come, he released himself and came with her . . .

"Did you leave someone behind recently?" she asked a little bit later.

"Why do you ask that?"

"You were more than hesitant in the lobby," she explained, "and then a little hesitant before we began. I'm not being immodest, but why else would you have to think twice about my offer?"

"I *was* with someone recently, yes."

"Married?"

"No."

"Did you love her?"

"She asked me that, too."

"And what was your answer?"

"I never gave her a straight answer."

She snuggled into the crook of his arm and said, "You should go back, even if it's just to give it to her straight. She deserves that."

"Yes, you're right," Clint said. "She does."

"She's going to be sorry to lose you, though," Sherry said, sleepily. "I can't say that I blame her for that."

"Go to sleep," he said, but it was unnecessary advice.

She was already asleep.

THIRTY-FIVE

Clint woke early the next morning and rolled out of bed without waking Sherry. She looked a lot younger in repose, and for a moment he had the uncomfortable feeling that he might have bedded a seventeen-year-old girl, or younger. Looking at the shapely form beneath the sheet, however, that fear quickly faded away.

He dressed and packed without her stirring. He looked at her then, briefly wondering if he should leave her a note, but what would he say? He simply left, closing the door quietly behind him.

Downstairs he checked out, then laid some extra money on the clerk/owner.

"What's this for?"

"There's a young lady asleep in my room," Clint said.

"I don't want her disturbed until she's good and ready to get up. Understand?"

The man gave Clint his knowingest smile and said, "I understand, Mr. Adams. I hope you had a pleasant night."

"And take this for her room," Clint said, handing over enough money to cover Sherry's room, as well.

"Thank you."

Clint put his forefinger beneath the man's nose and said, "Don't try charging her for the night."

Looking shocked the man said, "Excuse me, Mr. Adams, but—"

"Spare me the outrage, partner," Clint said. "Maybe I've just got a suspicious nature. If I'm wrong, I apologize, but just remember what I said."

Clint picked up his saddlebags and rifle and left the hotel, heading for the livery.

Saddling his horse he thought about Caroline and Amanda Fleming, and realized that it was the first time he'd thought about them since he tumbled into bed with Sherry Logan. That was a good sign, and he wished he could wake Sherry and thank her for that, but it was time to move on.

Johnny Robak was moving his way and pretty soon their paths would cross again.

Sherry Logan woke two hours after Clint Adams had gone. She felt his side of the bed, and it was already cool, so she knew there was no catching him before he left.

She rose and went to her own room, where she dressed quickly, putting on a shirt and jeans. Even though he had already left, there was a possibility that she could pick up his trail. She stopped short, with one boot on and one boot off, and thought, Who am I kidding? She was no tracker, but maybe she could at least find out what direction he had gone in.

She didn't want to lose contact with him now that she had found him. She was tired of being teased by her male colleagues in the newspaper business, always being given the unexciting stories to work on. The first time she'd laid eyes on Clint Adams—even though he'd been naked—she'd recognized him as the Gunsmith. She knew that almost two months ago he'd been outdrawn for the first time, because she'd read the stories, but no one had gotten an exclusive interview with him. Her difficulty in the hotel lobby had been genuine, but the Gunsmith coming to her rescue had been a godsend.

After he'd saved her she had left the hotel and gone directly to the telegraph office. She had sent her editor on the *Sante Fe Gazette* word that she was on the trail of a hot interview, and that she'd keep in touch. Next, she planned her approach to Clint Adams.

Obviously, he was the damsel-in-distress type, and she decided to try and play on that part of his character.

Her original intention had been to try and interview him at dinner, treating the fact that she was a newspaper reporter as a coincidence. When she hadn't been able to bring it up during the meal, she decided to go back to his room with him.

Now, that decision had not been made totally with emotion. Admittedly, she was excited by him, and wanted to go to bed with him, but she had not expected to be so overwhelmed by having sex with him that she would fall into an exhausted sleep and forget about her original goal.

When she was finally dressed she grabbed her carpet bag and hurried from the room to go downstairs and check out. The desk clerk told her that the room fee had already been taken care of, by Mr. Adams.

"How long ago did he leave?" she asked.

"About two hours."

"Did he say where he was headed?"

"No, he didn't."

"Thanks."

"Will you be leaving us, miss?"

"Oh, yes . . ." she said over her shoulder as she rushed out.

She hurried to the livery and found out from the man there which direction Clint had gone in. He was headed south. Since she'd arrived in town by stage she dickered with the man over renting a horse, and then left town, heading south.

She was a fairly accomplished rider, but never having ridden the trail before, she left without so much as a piece of beef jerky.

She wouldn't think about that until later, though. Right now all she had in mind was her story, not her stomach.

THIRTY-SIX

Clint was pouring himself a second cup of coffee when he heard the approaching rider, who was obviously making no attempt to be silent.

"Hello!" he heard a woman's voice call out, and he thought he recognized it. "Hello the fire!"

"Come ahead," he called back.

He heard the rider start forward again, and then she came into view, entering the circle of light thrown by his campfire.

"Sherry?" he said, staring at her in disbelief.

"Clint," she said, dismounting. She walked her horse closer and said contritely, "Don't be mad at me, please."

"Why would I be mad at you?" he asked.

"You might," she said, "when I tell you what I'm doing here."

171

"Why?" he asked. "What are you doing here?"

"Before I go into that, could I have a cup of coffee and something to eat? I'm starved."

"Don't you have any supplies?"

"I'm afraid I didn't think that far ahead."

He took her reins from her and said, "I'll take care of your horse. All I have to eat is beef jerky, but you can wash it down with the coffee."

"I'll take what I can get," she said gratefully.

He unsaddled her horse and cared for him before joining her at the fire.

"Where'd you get that piece of crowbait?" he asked.

"I rented him," she said, chewing on a piece of jerky.

"I hope you didn't pay too much."

"I dickered a bit, but I was in too much of a hurry to leave."

"Want to tell me about that now?"

She sipped her coffee and eyed him over the rim of the cup.

"All right," she said, "but try to understand and not get mad."

"I'm a very understanding guy," he assured her.

She hesitated, as if she had her doubts, and then started talking . . .

When she finished Clint picked up the coffeepot and poured himself the last cup of coffee in it.

"Well?" she asked.

"Well, what?"

"Are you mad?"

"Maybe I should be," he said, sipping his coffee, "but I'm not."

"You're not?" she asked, in surprise.

"No."

"How come?"

"Because you were doing your job," he said, "at least, up to a point—I hope."

"Oh, yes," she said hurriedly. "I mean, I thought I could maybe get into your bed and you'd talk to me, but once you . . . you touched me, I forgot why I was there."

"That's nice," he said.

"It's true!"

"I said it was nice."

"You said, 'That's nice,' " she said, mimicking his tone. "Which means, 'That's nice . . . *if* it's true.' "

He finished his coffee and then emptied the dregs from the pot to the fire.

"Better get some sleep," he said. "I want to get an early start in the morning."

"Clint!" she said, standing up.

"What?"

"How about it?"

"How about what?"

"An interview!"

"I don't give interviews, Sherry—is that your name?"

"Of course that's my name."

"Well, I just wondered, that's all."

"You don't believe a word I've said."

"Sure I do."

"What?" she demanded. "What do you believe?"

"I believe that you work for a newspaper, and I believe that you enjoyed yourself last night."

"How do you know that?" she asked, belligerently.

"Because I enjoyed myself."

The look on her face softened and she said, "Oh, of course I enjoyed it, but I'd still like to have that interview."

"I told you, I don't do interviews."

"Well then, we'll make it a profile."

"What's a profile?"

"I'll ask questions and you'll answer them, but when I write it up it won't be question and answer, it'll be . . . well, a profile."

"If that ain't an interview, I don't know what it is."

"It's a profile," she said stubbornly.

"Well, no interviews, and no profiles. We'll start out early in the morning and ride together to the next town. From there we go our separate ways . . . and don't think it hasn't been nice."

"You—" she said.

"Your saddle is over there," he said, gesturing. "Make yourself comfortable. I'll wake you at first light."

"Who's gonna wake you?" she said glumly.

"I don't need anybody to wake me," he said. "I'll wake up."

Clint laid down and made himself comfortable, tipped his hat down low over his eyes and tried to go to sleep.

"Clint?"

"What?"

"Did that man really beat you?"

"That question is in the form of an interview, isn't it?"

"Damn you, I'm just asking you a question."

There was no reply.

"Are you asleep?"

No answer.

"Where are you headed now that you're all healed up?"

Nothing.

"Are you trying to find him, this Johnny Robak? To finally decide who's best?"

When she said it that way it sounded silly. "To finally decide who's best" like it was a contest, a boxing match, or something.

"Clint—"

"Go to sleep, Sherry. Just go to sleep."

He wasn't looking for Robak to find out who was best. He was just doing what Sherry would do if she made a mistake in a story she was writing.

He was erasing his mistake.

THIRTY-SEVEN

The next morning Clint and Sherry rode into Gainsville, New Mexico. Clint hadn't realized it when he camped, but he'd only been two hours from town.

Sherry had tried to approach the question of an interview on several occasions during the morning ride, but Clint had never even deigned to discuss it.

"You are the stubbornest man I ever met, and I've met some stubborn men."

"Girl your age can't have met that many men."

"I'm twenty-four!"

"You act younger."

"You didn't complain in your hotel room!"

Clint didn't comment on that.

They rode to the livery stable, where they left their horses.

"What are you going to do now?"

"I'm going to get some food inside of me."

"When will you be leaving?"

"First thing in the morning."

"Are you going to take a hotel room?"

"I am," he said, "and I'm not going to be letting anyone else in."

"Why you—" she said, but he quickened his pace and she had to run to catch up.

At the hotel he checked in, and then she checked in right after him. He went upstairs without pausing to see what room she was in. Once he was in his room he removed his boots and rubbed his feet. After staying in one place for so long, and losing weight due to his wound, it would take him a while to build himself up to the point where he could take traveling as well as he used to.

He walked to his window, which overlooked the main street, and wondered how far away Johnny Robak was.

Robak broke camp at first light and headed for the next town. He wanted a hot meal, a hot bath, and a hot, willing woman. It would take him four hours to reach town, by which time there would still be time for breakfast.

As he saddled up he tried to remember what the fella back in Tucumcari had said the name of the next town was.

Oh, yeah, now he remembered.

It was Gainsville.

Sherry tried resting in her hotel room, wondering if Clint would come, wondering if she should go to him—

wishing she had the nerve to go to him.

She still had today and tomorrow to try and convince him to give her an interview. If he still refused, she doubted that she would be bold enough to follow him again.

If she was willing to give up that easily, maybe she was in the wrong business.

Clint went to the saloon just after noon for a cold beer. It was a little early, but his chest was aching. He knew a cold beer wouldn't soothe the ache, but maybe he could pretend it would.

He ordered his beer and then took the farthest table from the door of the almost-empty saloon.

He thought about Sherry Logan. She'd been surprised that he hadn't been openly angry with her and frankly, so had he. It was true, though, that she had only been trying to do her job. He wished he could help her, but he just wasn't willing to talk to anyone about what had happened with Johnny Robak.

Not yet.

After noon Sherry decided to leave her room and find Clint. She had to keep trying as long as she could. An interview with him would mean a lot to her career.

Not getting it could mean the end of it.

Johnny Robak rode into Gainsville just after noon. The first thing he wanted after putting his horse up in the livery—even before a bath, a meal, or a woman—was a cold beer.

He was walking to the saloon when he saw the woman walking ahead of him. She was wearing jeans and he watched her tight butt with pleasure as she continued ahead of him. He was surprised to see her enter the saloon, and quickened his pace.

Maybe he could kill two birds with one beer.

Sherry spotted Clint as soon as she walked into the saloon. It was easy, there were only two other men there, and one was the bartender.

Clint saw her and tightened his hand around his beer mug. His patience would only extend so far. He hoped he still had some slack left.

"Clint—" she said, sitting across from him, but she stopped short when she saw the look on his face as he looked past her.

She turned in her seat and saw a man standing just inside the batwing doors, and he was staring at Clint.

Robak entered the saloon, and when he saw the man that the woman sat with, his heartbeat quickened.

This was going to be the best damned beer he ever tasted.

He went to the bar, ordered the beer, and then walked to Clint's table.

THIRTY-EIGHT

"What a coincidence," Robak said.

"No coincidence, Robak," Clint said.

Sherry looked from one man to the other and started breathing faster. This was even better than an interview. The mere fact that she happened to be present when these two men met again was like an omen to her.

"Don't tell me you're looking for me," Robak said.

"That's right."

"Want to try me again?" Robak asked. "Didn't get enough last time?"

"This time," Clint said, "there won't be any little girls in the way."

"Is that your excuse for last time?"

Robak looked at Sherry then and put his hand on the back of her neck.

"This your friend?" he asked Clint.

"That's right," she said, batting Robak's hand away, "we're friends."

"Well," Robak said, "when I'm finished with your friend, I'll come back, and you and I can get better acquainted."

Robak finished his beer and slammed the empty mug down on the table with a loud bang that made Sherry jump.

"On the street," he said to Clint, and then turned and left the saloon.

Sherry watched Clint as he leisurely sipped his beer.

"That was him, huh?"

"That was him."

"Are you afraid to go out there?"

Clint smiled at her and said, "Is this in the way of an interview?"

"Damn you, Clint—"

"You've got something better than an interview now, Sherry," he said, pushing his seat back. "You've got a front row seat."

He stood up and started for the door. When he heard her rise he turned and said, "Stay inside, Sherry. You can watch, but just stay inside."

"All right," she said.

Clint nodded, then went to the batwing doors and stepped outside.

Robak was standing in the street to his left, waiting for him. Apparently no one had noticed anything strange yet, because there were no onlookers. Clint stepped into the street, hoping that this would be over before a crowd could gather.

He started forward as if he were simply crossing the street but stopped right in the center and turned to face Robak.

This was the first time in a long time that he was facing a man he wanted desperately to kill.

"After you," Robak said.

Clint took him up on the offer.

As his hand streaked for his gun he felt an ache in his chest that made him nauseated. He ignored it and eased his gun from his holster cleanly, smoothly.

Suddenly Robak knew he'd made a mistake. He grabbed for his gun, but he knew it was too late.

He was a dead man.

Sherry watched from behind the batwing doors, and even though she was watching, she hardly saw Clint move when suddenly his gun was in his hand and he fired, once. The bullet hit Robak squarely in the chest, and she saw blood burst forth from the wound.

Robak stood stock-still after taking a forced step back, and then it was as if someone had cut his legs out from beneath him. He simply crumpled to the ground, as if all his bones had turned to water.

Clint walked to Robak and stood over him for a moment, and the townspeople, as if just discovering what had happened, began to gather. Clint turned away from the body just before a crowd encircled it.

He walked to where Sherry was standing, took a moment to replace the spent round in his gun, and then holstered it.

"Was that better than an interview?" he asked.

She didn't answer. Her throat seemed to have closed up on her.

"Is this the first time you've seen a man die?"

She nodded.

"Not a pretty sight, is it?"

She shook her head, wondering again if she was in the right business.

"Well," he said, looking off at something only he could see, "I guess I won't wait until tomorrow to leave. I've got to go back the way I came." He was thinking about Caroline and Amanda.

He looked at her, and when she still didn't say anything, he turned and started for the livery.

She cleared her throat with an effort and called out, "Clint?"

He turned and said, "Yes?"

"How—how does it feel to be the Gunsmith again?"

"Honey," he said to her, "you really are in the right business."

From the *Santa Fe Gazette,* by Sherry Logan:

   . . . Clint Adams' hand moved faster than the eye could possibly follow, and his gun sounded once. The bullet struck Robak in the center of the chest, sending forth a spurt of blood. Robak stood stock-still for a moment, his gun still in its holster, then he crumpled to the ground, dead.

   Clint Adams, on this day, had once again become "The Gunsmith."

   The legend is back!

Watch for

SIX-GUN JUSTICE

eighty-first novel in the
exciting GUNSMITH series

coming in September!

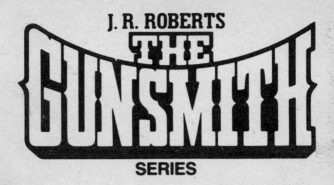

J. R. ROBERTS
THE GUNSMITH
SERIES